SHIP OF DEATH

I made a rapid circuit of the main deck. Aunt Kathleen was ensconced in a deck chair, her green cape billowing in the wind which was vigorously chasing white clouds across a deep blue sky. She waved to me and I quickly settled myself beside her.

"'Tis a grand day, Brian, wouldn't you say? We've been needing a bit of wind to clear the cobwebs from our brains. I hope you slept well?"

"Not too well, Aunt Kathleen. Attempted murder doesn't exactly encourage sweet dreams."

"Attempted murder is it? Do you mean you're writing a thriller? A waste of your satirical talents, if you ask me."

I was in no mood for another sympathetic discussion of my alleged talents. "I'm not writing anything," I told her. "This was a real life attempt. Or maybe I should say a 'real death attempt.' *On me!*"

FIVE PORTS TO DANGER

VIVIAN CONNOLLY

Book Margins, Inc.

A BMI Edition

Published by special arrangement with Dorchester
Publishing Co., Inc.

Printed in the United States of America.

FIVE PORTS TO DANGER

CHAPTER 1

The funny little brass band was playing a *paso doble*, the same one I'd heard last Sunday in Cordova when the matadors entered the bullring. This wasn't an entrance, though. It was an exit. An exit in the grand style. That was one of the things I liked about Spaniards. They did everything with class. The *Virgen de Toluca* was not the *Queen Elizabeth*. She was smaller and had a potbellied look about her. Her paint was dingy, and some of her life preservers carried the name of her sister ship, the *Monserrat*. Still, dowdy and haphazard as she might be, she rated a *muy grande* send-off. The band, flags all over the place, flowers by the ton, happy passengers lining the railings, weeping relatives on the dock, everybody waving white handkerchiefs, earsplitting blasts on the whistle, the whole bit. A classic scene. I felt like a character in a movie made around 1938.

The last man hurrying up the gangplank looked like a fellow actor in my movie. He wore a belted black trench coat and had a wide-brimmed felt hat pulled low over his face as if he was ashamed of his looks. He wasn't waving to anybody, and he didn't linger by the railing. He practically snatched his ticket back out of the hands of the dude with the gold braid, pushed his way through the crowd around the top of the gangplank, and disappeared. Bogart would have done the whole thing more casually. This guy would never make it with Twentieth Century Fox.

I thought about how nice it would be if I were back in the Thirties. Then I could be Dashiell Hammett and save myself all the wear and tear that went with being Brian Singdahlsen. My American publisher might even stop remaindering my books. I wouldn't be maundering around trying to decide if I ought to junk my so-called style and dream up a new one.

That was what this trip was supposed to do for me, give me a whole new slant on life. And writing, naturally. I hadn't reached the point yet where life without writing seemed possible. If things kept progressing downward at the present rate, that day might come. It was great to know my first novel was currently a best seller in Finland, but eventually I might run out of literate Finns. *Eating*, which had made quite a splash at first, had already disappeared from any conceivable American bookshop. I couldn't even find a copy for the rare admirer who wanted to pay cash for one instead of borrowing it from me or a library.

The two books that followed *Eating* hadn't even made it through a third printing. Of course, if Peter could get that Finnish translator to sober up, I might still get lunch money from one of them. But the omens were ominous. At least, my British publishers didn't remainder my books. They kept everything they'd ever printed stacked neatly away in some old warehouse down by the Thames. I'd never been there, but the betting was good they'd still have some of Marie Corelli's weaker efforts tucked away in one of the corners, the covers tastefully decorated with the tooth-marks of an intellectual river rat. My books bided their time there patiently. One of these days the underground wave of adulation for Singdahlsen's early works would surface, and then both Peter Leyton and I would make a pretty penny selling first editions at astronomical prices.

This whole sea voyage caper had been Peter's idea. I remembered that talk over a pub lunch in London five weeks before. I'd been sounding off to good old Peter, my British editor, about all my assorted woes.

"It would seem you've gone stale for the moment, Brian. Don't worry. It happens to every writer. It happened to Hemingway."

"Hemingway's dead," I said. "He doesn't have to eat any more. I do."

"You really do have this oral fixation, don't you?"

"Stop talking like a C.C.N.Y. sophomore," I said. "Sympathize! Here I am, a black humor writer with a white skin who's lost his comic touch. What chance have I got? Maybe I should forget the whole satire thing. When *Eating* came out, it seemed pretty funny to have a guy living in a converted sewer with a hidden entrance to a supermarket. Now it sounds like a practical way to fight inflation. My material keeps bouncing out of my head and into real life. Facts are a lot funnier than fiction these days."

"Just because you had the bad luck to get yourself so involved in that novel about a computerized robot who is elected President of the United States . . ."

"Yeah, how about that? My brilliant idea has become a cartoonist's cliché. Peter, I've got to find some new approach. Satire just doesn't make it any more."

"I don't believe that. I still think you're simply at low tide right now. You'll come out of this funk, and your work will be better than ever. I don't think I have to tell you again how highly I regard you as a writer."

"You don't have to, but it might help," I said.

Peter's eyes brightened. "I'll give you more than kind words. I'll give you some advice on how to get over this bad spell. Get out of London. You're getting too tangled up in the literary rat race here. I've watched it happening. Do you know, you're even developing a British accent."

"Gorblimey!"

"Seriously, you are. It's a bad sign. Too many outside influences."

"Seriously, you might be right." I thought about the outside influences, one in particular. Her name was Margo. She was a girl with whom I intermittently exchanged insults and physical raptures. Ostensibly, her job was secretary to a public relations firm. Her real vocation was the strenuous work involved in remaining "with it" in swinging London, where the definition of "in" and "out" changed daily, or sometimes, hourly.

In some ways, Margo was the ideal female for the semi-detached arrangement that seemed to suit me at the moment. With her I didn't have to worry about sudden lapses into "I'm really old-fashioned enough to believe in marriage." She was good in bed. She could cook pretty well, which is a fantastically rare quality among English girls.

But there was always this feeling that wherever we were, and whatever we were doing, she was checking us out against the catalog in her head to see if this was really the sort of thing a swinging London chick should be doing. Discotheques, sure. Quiet evenings at home, maybe, so long as there was a constant accompaniment from the latest pop record. American writer with name frequently mentioned in public press, fine. American writer struggling to produce next masterpiece—semi-acceptable. American writer fading into obscurity—better start looking for replacement. That was about the point we'd reached, where I was neither "in" nor "out," and the feeling was not one of utmost comfort. Yes, leaving London for awhile might be a good idea.

"The trouble is," I told Peter, "I don't know where

to go. There's a rat race everywhere, and I'm just the kind of guy who always gets hung up in it.''

"How about a Greek island?''

"I've tried that. By the second week, everybody on the island was my lifelong friend and I spent all my time drinking *retsina* in waterfront cafes.''

"Have yourself dropped by helicopter in the Amazon.''

"A neat scheme,'' I said admiringly. "But I'm too damn civilized. I like a hot shower and a cold beer every day. Besides, real solitude would drive me up the wall. I like to have people around me, chattering to each other, walking around, picking their noses. I like to look up from my scribbling and watch them. I just don't want them to talk to me. That's where all the trouble starts.''

Peter looked thoughtfully at the remnants of his slice of prime rib. Then his eyes narrowed. That was a sure sign his brain had shifted into high.

"Do you speak any Spanish?'' he asked.

"*Chinga su madre*,'' I said.

Peter flushed. "There's no need to get personal, Brian.''

"I'm quoting, not cussing,'' I said. "That's the only Spanish I know.''

Peter's smile came back. "Excellent,'' he said. "I know just the medicine you need. I'll take care of the whole thing. Can you meet me here for lunch on Thursday? I'll have all the arrangements laid on.''

"Wait a minute! Arrangements for what?''

"Brian, I assure you that in your present state of mind you must let me make the decisions. While you're this depressed, you'll have some bright objection to anything I suggest. You must simply put yourself in my hands and follow my instructions with complete and total faith in my judgment. I haven't failed you yet, have I?''

"I've got to admit you haven't."

"Then trust me now. Lunch here on Thursday, right?"

"So long as you're paying for it," I said. What the hell. Might as well humor him. At least, if his bright idea, whatever it was, turned out to be a bummer, I could blame Peter for a change. I was worn out from kicking myself in the ass all the time.

When Thursday lunchtime came round, Peter was as close to bubbling with excitement as I'd ever seen him. As soon as we'd ordered, he pulled a manila envelope out of his attache case and handed it to me. I yanked some printed papers out of it. A small object fell and hit the pub floor with a metallic clink. I picked it up. It was a key.

"The key to the flat a rich friend of mine keeps in Marbella," said Peter, beaming. "You can hole up there for a couple weeks before the *Virgen de Toluca* sails."

"Who or what is the *Virgen de Toluca*?"

"An ancient little passenger ship that sails from Cadiz, on the south coast of Spain, to Veracruz, Mexico," said Peter. "Emily and I made the trip a few years ago. Very relaxing. About two hundred passengers, all from Spain or Latin America. Nobody speaks English. Trip takes three weeks. Swimming pool, bars, dancing on the deck if you want it—not exactly posh, rather homely sort of atmosphere. Stops at the Canaries, Santo Domingo, Puerto Rico and Caracas en route—a little sightseeing to enliven the pleasant torpor."

"I'm going to be trapped on this overpopulated tub for three weeks?"

"I told you everyone will be speaking Spanish. You don't speak it."

"I didn't speak any Greek when I landed on that island," I said.

"The Spanish are different," said Peter. "More reserved. If you want to talk to them, that's fine, they'll be friendly. But if you want to preserve your solitude, they'll let you. I recommend the forward section of the main deck, right over the bow. No one ever comes there except an occasional crew member. Sea spray, gulls, salt breeze. Very invigorating."

It began to sound attractive. Three weeks before the mast. Chris Columbus' route, with me at the helm of the *Santa Maria*. Words like *intrepid, uncharted, vagabond*, swam through my mind.

"Behind him lay the grey Azores
Behind, the Gates of Hercules
Before him not the ghost of shores
Before him only shoreless seas,"

I quoted.

"I say, Brian, that's a rather nice bit of doggerel for spur-of-the-moment stuff," said Peter.

"Not my work," I admitted. "Tenth grade English at Pasadena High School. Some great American poet or other."

"Oh," said Peter damply. Then he perked up again. "You've stopped bloody objecting. Don't tell me you actually *like* my idea?"

"Sounds kind of different," I said. "What's all this paper?"

"There's a plane ticket to Marbella, your ticket for the boat, the address of my friend's flat and some tourist literature about Spain. The *Virgen* leaves Cadiz on March fifteenth. You'd better leave London immediately, before that quicksilver mind of yours goes sour on the idea. A few weeks of sun and seashore while you're waiting to sail won't hurt."

I looked at the standard drizzle outside. "Sun?" I asked incredulously.

"I told you you'd been in London too long. Yes, Brian, there still is a sun shining somewhere. In February, the *Costa del Sol* is a likely place to find it."

Peter's idea was sounding better and better. Then my beleaguered pessimism came to life and started to fight back.

"All very nice until I get to Veracruz," I said. "What then? Tell the conductor I left my galoshes in Spain and have to go back to get them?"

"A lot can happen in three weeks. Your mood may be very different by the time you land. In any case, Veracruz is a delightful old town. Festive, easygoing, marimba bands, beer for fivepence in sidewalk cafes under stone arcades, palm trees. . ."

"Let's skip your English romanticism about palm trees, Peter. Remember, I grew up in Los Angeles."

"Ah, but this is different. Palm trees without smog!"

"Tell me, when were you in Veracruz?"

"Oh. . .ten years or so ago."

"Want to place a small wager with some reliable bookmaker about that smog estimate?"

Peter suddenly became very businesslike. "Now look here, Brian, you're beginning to carp again. Stop it. You agreed to place yourself completely in my hands."

That was true. But the Singdahlsen pessimism does not give up easily. "You're forgetting one thing, Peter. How am I going to pay for this magnificent jaunt?"

"It's all laid on. We'll consider it an advance against future royalties. I assume your passport is in order?"

"Yeah, no problem there," I admitted. The magic word *advance* had delivered its usual body blow to the old pessimism. "O.K., Peter, I might as well relax and enjoy it. I'll send you a postcard from Veracruz. Or maybe even a manuscript." *Oh, oh, watch it,*

Singdahlsen, I told myself. *Euphoria is beginning to take over*. I struggled to hold on to my nice safe depression. The drizzle helped. So did the thought of packing.

As it turned out, the packing was no problem. Margo took care of most of it, along with things like getting the electricity and phone turned off. She seemed almost as relieved to be getting rid of me as I was at getting some distance between us. So after a relatively painless interval of three days, I found myself on an Air Iberia plane, winging southward, as they say in the ads.

Marbella had been nice. Most of the English-speaking jet-setters littering the beach around me were so rich I got stage fright at the thought of talking to them. I did pick up, in my usual magpie fashion, too many words of Spanish for my own good, but now I was on shipboard, I resolved to bury my new vocabulary and stick to "*No comprendo*" and pointing my finger at the menu.

While I'd been reliving all this stuff in my mind, the ship had cleared the harbor, and we were well out to sea. As if on cue, the word "menu" in my reverie was followed by the actual sound of a gong being struck, loudly and slowly. The sound seemed to move around the deck in a steady progress. Wondering how we had suddenly slipped out of Twentieth Century Fox into J. Arthur Rank, I looked to see where the sound was coming from. It turned out to be the work of a waiter in one of those little short white coats and shiny black pants. Evidently a lot of my fellow passengers already knew the drill, because they started streaming toward the back end of the ship. (I wasn't yet enough of a salty dog to use words like "stern" or "aft," even to myself.)

I followed them. They flowed down both sides of a branching staircase lined with gleaming oak bannisters to the deck below. As I'd guessed, it was the dining room. I saw at once what Peter had meant by "homely," in the English sense. Though there were a few small tables for four, the others were very long affairs seating ten or twelve people. My eagle eye picked up some patches in the heavy white tablecloths. It also picked up the welcome sight of large decanters of red wine deployed at pleasantly close intervals on the table. Peter had told me the bar prices would be low, but he'd neglected to mention the free wine. There didn't seem to be any bureaucratic hang-ups about where to sit, so I followed the example of the other people and plopped myself down in the first empty chair I came to.

Dinner was good. It meandered on for about seven courses, and some of the courses had two choices. I quickly worked out a system of sign language with the waiter. For fish, he'd make swimming motions with his hands; for fowl, he'd flap his elbows; for meat, he'd put his fingers to his head like horns. The system was simple, logical and consistent, and it gave the rest of the people at the table so much entertainment that they soon quit trying to teach me Spanish.

There were eight other people at the table, including two very well-behaved kids, a boy about eight and a girl about eleven. These were attached to a set of parents who looked bored enough with each other to make it a safe bet they'd been married about twenty years. There was another married couple, a little older and pudgier. The rest were all unattached males. At the foot of the table sat a dark-haired man of about twenty-eight or so, his hair sleeked back in that Valentino style that people like bank clerks and police chiefs still wear in Spain. He seemed nervous. His dark eyes kept glancing around the dining room, as if he was looking for someone he didn't especially want to see. He didn't look at anybody at our table, just applied himself to the food as if he was afraid the cook might run out of supplies half way across the ocean. He skipped dessert (that nice custard thing I had already become addicted to in Spain) and left the table early. In his own way, he seemed to be trying on the same hermit bit as I was, only he was more surly about it. I, at least, gave them a big smile every time I said, "*No comprendo*."

The man across from me was about my age and build. However, he was a much jollier type than I am. He had a boyish face and curly brown hair which he let flop around a little, and apparently liked kids. Anyway, he immediately set up what sounded like a conversation full of fun and teasing with the boy and girl, which started them sparkling and chattering, while mom and pop beamed happily over the whole scene. The other couple smiled benignly too.

The only person who didn't seem to be charmed with the boyish dude's performance was the guy beside me, a tall young character built like a surfer, with pimples and shoulder-length black hair, wearing a mod shirt and purple bell-bottoms. He glowered a little at the sunshine-spreader across from us and said something about him to me in Spanish which sounded pretty derogatory. I pulled my *No comprendo* act, which at first looked like it was going to be a bad mistake, because this guy spoke English. Or thought he did. It turned out to be largely a false alarm. He wasn't able to get across to me what was so lousy about the dude across from us, though he managed, with sign language and a few assorted English words to tell me why he thought *he* was so great.

"Me, *actore*," he said, pointing at himself and beaming. "Wow, berry O.K. *Pero* no yob in Mexico. No is *Grew Bee*. Me *a Espana*." He waved his hands to signify flying. "May be yob in *Espana*. Wow, no *bueno*. Me *regreso a* Mexico. May be *Grew Bee* today."

I was catching all of this except the "*Grew Bee* bit, but I was definitely not in the market for a lifelong friendship with this twerp, who struck me as the kind of

17

loser who has a way of latching on to me and becoming impossible to shake, short of premeditated murder. So I stuck to a vague, bewildered stare. After awhile, the character gave up on me and started a charm contest with the guy across from us. He soon had the older couple laughing and talking, the husband clinking wine glasses with him, so maybe he was less of a loser when he stuck to Spanish.

I realized that mealtimes on the *Virgen de Toluca* were not going to be the social highlights of my day. Well, that was what I wanted, wasn't it? To be left alone? Still, I might at least have chosen a table with a pretty girl to look at. Good for the digestion.

I glanced around the crowded dining room. Most of the women were attached to kids or definitely middle aged. A few were positively ancient. The two who didn't fit those categories looked even more spectacular by contrast.

The one I spotted first was spectacular in the show-biz sense of the word. It was no accident that my ocular reconnaissance came to a screeching halt at her table, over in one corner. She invited lengthy inspection. She was wearing a bright flower print, one of those long slinky affairs which reveals everything it's ostensibly covering up. She had the sort of figure I associate with names like Lillian Russell, very slim waist with breath-taking curves above and below. Her dark shoulder-length hair was loose and wavy. Her black eyes would probably have been fascinating enough without the professional framing job she'd done on them. With eyeshadow and all that gup, she was a match for the earlier vintage Elizabeth Taylor, and she had a tableful of enchanted males to prove it. She knew how to use those eyes and that body; just the right combination of sexiness and remoteness. She had them hanging on her every word and movement, all except one, a hefty black-mustached character in a white shirt, black linen blazer and baby-blue bow tie, who leaned back in amused proprietary fashion. Husband or boyfriend, no doubt, savoring the prestige of possession.

I don't usually go to these luxuriant females, but this one was different. She seemed to be enjoying herself so much, as if she understood that sex could be a hilarious practical joke. There was none of the usual bitchiness or narcissism about the way she came on; she looked like an expert entertainer who enjoyed doing her act well. In my mind I named her "Carmen." I thought she might be a nice person to know, and not only in the Biblical sense.

After I'd spent most of the meat course taking her in, I turned my eyes loose on the room at large again. That's when I saw the second girl, at the table which ran parallel with my own. She was not nearly so obvious as Carmen. She was wearing a rather severe little dark suit thing, with a lacy froth at the neckline. Her hair was piled on her head in a sleek black shiny mound. It was the way she held herself that got to me first—graceful, assured, back straight, not too stiff. Then, as she leaned forward in my direction to talk to someone across the table from her, I got a good look at her eyes. They were blue, almost lavender. My weeks in Spain had shaken me out of the stereotype that all Spaniards have dark eyes, but in her case it was more than novelty that made her eyes exceptional. No window dressing this time— maybe a touch of eyeshadow, but nothing a London swinger like Margo would have dignified with the name of make-up. I was just moving my appreciative gaze down to check the rest of the equipment—a delicate acquiline nose, clear white skin—when she became aware of my stare and pointedly turned to the old woman beside her and began an animated conversation.

For some absurd reason, I felt like a peeping Tom

caught in the act. "For Chrissake, lady," I wanted to say, "I was only looking." I noticed that the actor character next to me was doing his share of looking too. Being stared at by predatory males could surely be nothing new to her. All the same, galloping discretion set in, and I sailed through the vegetables and custard with never another glance in her direction. Subtlety was the key here, I told myself. That I had plenty of. I was often so subtle in my approaches that an amazingly large number of women couldn't remember ever having met me.

I brought my lascivious reverie to a sharp close. What the hell was I doing? Here I was, having chosen the equivalent of a desert island so I could get back in touch with myself, and already I was casing the joint for dames. That was no way to stay out of the rat race. I should be absorbing all kinds of new ambiances, observing different character types, a detached bystander on the look for material. *I am a camera*, I plagiarized softly to myself, *simply recording, a blank tablet waiting for life to make its impression. . .*

The joker who periodically shares my head with me came back with the punch line: *A camera is right. You're an instamatic. Always set for the same speed and exposure. No wonder you're in a rut.*

Now that was unfair. I'd been doing the observation bit all afternoon. How about those clever thoughts I'd been having about the last man aboard and Humprey Bogart? I looked around the dining room to see if I could spot the man in the black trench coat. I hadn't seen much of his face, and his build was pretty much like your standard Spaniard—maybe a little less chunky, a little skinnier—more like my own, in fact. Very like my own. About the same height, five eleven, with shoulders neither broad nor narrow. We were both pretty unmemorable specimens, I decided. Probably he'd make an even less interesting character in a book than I would myself.

I shook off the familiar first symptoms of the descent to the abyss, and decided to take a walk on deck, looking for that neat isolated spot Peter had told me about. It had turned dark and a little chilly, so I went back to my cabin for my windbreaker. I had already stowed away my suitcase there earlier. At that point, none of the other three bunks had been occupied, so I had taken the lower bunk nearest the porthole. Now, as I opened the door, I saw I had acquired a cabin mate. A square-faced man with a brush cut wearing a dark suit was sitting on the bunk across from mine, lapping up the last of a dish of custard. I took in the black trenchcoat lying beside him on the bunk and the soft felt hat tossed on the upper berth. So that was why I hadn't spotted him in the dining room. He'd been eating his dinner off a tray here.

He looked up as I came in, shoved his tray aside, stood up and did that thing that would be a heel click if a German did it, but is something else again in Spain. "Raoul Alvarez Paredo," he said, with a little nod of his head.

"Brian Singdahlsen," I answered, without trying to imitate his choreography. We stood looking at each other a minute. Then I said, *"No hablo espanol."* Instead of looking sorry to hear I didn't speak Spanish, as most Spaniards did, he suddenly grinned broadly and said enthusiastically, with a flash of white teeth, *"Bueno! No hablo ingles!"* Then he kind of waved his hand airily at me, shifted the empty tray to the top bunk, plopped himself on his mattress and dug into a Spanish paperback, ignoring me completely.

Was I being put down? I hadn't yet tuned in well enough to the Spanish wavelength to be sure. In any case, it was solitude I had asked for, and by God, I was getting it. I picked up my windbreaker and went out on the deck.

It didn't take long to find the spot Peter had mentioned. On both of the rear tourist clask decks families and couples hung over the rails or lay back in deck chairs, picking out the stars which were now punching their way through holes in the black velvet sky. As I went forward on the main deck, they thinned out, and after I had picked my way through a collection of big wooden barrels and assorted packing crates, I found the small triangle of deck over the bow empty enough. I sat on one of those things they tie ropes around, and stared out ahead. Sure enough, there was nothing there but ocean! The bustle of passengers seemed miles behind me. Alone. I had made it! Alone with the universe. I didn't know how the universe felt about it, but it suited me just fine.

Of course it was too good to last. After about ten minutes of gazing out to infinity, I heard voices behind me. They weren't loud, but they were penetrating. They belonged to a man and a woman. Both of them sounded pretty emotional. They were talking in very rapid Spanish, so I couldn't understand a thing, though I was sure they were angry. They were hidden from me by one of the packing cases, so I couldn't see what they looked like.

I wanted to tell them to fuck off and leave me and my universe alone together, and I thought I knew just enough Spanish for that. But that would have meant instant involvement, which I theoretically didn't want. So I did the next best thing and tried to move unobtrusively away to look for a quieter spot.

Whereupon I tripped over a rope and obtruded sprawlingly into their scene. I caught myself before my head hit the deck and managed to look up at them. The woman was delightfully familiar—the blue-eyed beauty from the next table. I found myself quoting the would-be actor: "Wow!" Not subtle, this scene, but maybe an introduction—lovely aristocratic señorita succoring wounded stranger. Not anything I'd allow in a script of mine, but Twentieth Century Fox might buy it.

No such luck. As I lay there semi-stunned, whether by concussion or the possibilities I'm still not sure, the guy who'd been arguing with her grabbed the girl by the arm and hustled her away. I caught a quick glimpse of his face. I was almost sure it was the jolly boyish child-lover who'd sat across from me at dinner. Could it be? What a change of image. Now he was anything but charming. He was hissing nastily in Spanish at my Dulcinea, as she had instantly become. And he was being positively rough as he hauled her away from me into the darkness. Was she tied up with this creep somehow? Had I interrupted a lover's quarrel? Was this one of those "some enchanted evening" incidents doomed to a sudden death because the other party was already spoken for?

I dragged myself wearily to my feet. Vertical once more, I began to feel more hopeful. Judging by that scene, my competition wasn't all that much fun to be with. Certainly not subtle. *Subtlety's the key, Singdahlsen*, I repeated to myself. *I'm surer than ever*. Subtlety, tact, chivalry—was I not well equipped with all those sterling qualities? I didn't bother to scold myself for betraying that incipient entente between me and the universe with my thoughts of girl-catching. So far on the *Virgen de Toluca* everyone interesting had done a masterful job of avoiding me—first my cabin mate, now my new-found love, dragged about by this Jekyll-and-Hyde children's entertainer. All of a sudden I wasn't sure I needed all that much solitude.

CHAPTER 2

When I woke next morning, the fabled Singdahlsen will power was in the saddle again. This was a crisis in my life. There must be no wavering. My shell of solitude would remain impregnable.

My cabin mate, Raoul, was still sleeping. I looked at his square, tanned face in the early sunlight coming through the porthole. There was something strange and splotchy about it. Then I realized what it was. The skin of his chin and above his upper lip was lighter than the rest of his face. I remembered the time on the Greek island when I'd shaved off my six months growth of beard. I'd looked kind of strange myself for a few days.

So Raoul had recently jettisoned a beard and mustache. Well, so what? They wouldn't have fitted in with that Bogart role anyway.

I went up on deck. The sun was bright on the horizon behind us. I went aft (my language growing saltier) to watch the pretty colors it made on the sea. I climbed down a ladder to a lower deck I hadn't yet seen. It was the deck nearest to the water, partially enclosed, free of deck chairs but full of cargo. I looked at the labels on the barrels. Sherry, olives, sardines—those were easy, but what were *alcaparras*?

A sudden triumphant cock-a-doodle-do hit my

eardrums. What the hell? I eased myself around the barrels of *alcaparras* to the other side of the deck. I saw where the noise came from. There were about twenty wooden cages, piled on top of each other and lashed securely together with rope. In each cage stood a magnificent rooster, with scarlet comb and wattles, and feathers flashing purple, bronze, green and red in the early sun.

Standing by one of the cages, looking intently at its inmate, was the children's entertainer who had been so nasty to my Dulcinea last night. He looked up as I approached. Apparently he was back into the Doctor Jekyll role, for he beamed when he saw me, boyish charm smeared all over his face, and offered me a Chiclet. I shook my head, smiling too, and wondered if he recognized me as the guy who'd broken up his angry tete-a-tete last night. He didn't seem nervous or embarrassed, so I guessed he hadn't spotted me. I stuck determinedly to the *no comprendo* bit, and in a little while he strolled off, leaving me alone with the roosters.

I'm strictly a city boy, but I'd spent some summers on a farm near Petaluma, so chickens were no big thing for me. But I'd never seen any chickens like these. Those dumb bleating little clumps of freezer fodder in California were a whole different breed. These chickens oozed Soul! *Machismo*! Rooster Power! I could feel unkown hormones in me beginning to sizzle just looking at them.

"*Son magnificos, no?*" a deep voice boomed behind me. I turned quickly. The man praising the roosters was the right shape to play Sancho Panza to my Quixote, short and squat, with powerful chest and shoulders. But there was a smell of wealth about him that told me he was nobody's servant. He was wearing tan gabardine slacks and a snowy-white long-sleeved *guayabera*, one of those classy shirts with all the tucks and stitching and pearl buttons that is standard equipment for the well-dressed man of the Carribean. He had a round brown face with a rugged chin, a strong piratical nose and beetling pepper-and-salt eyebrows. His jet black hair looked as though his own personal barber had been at work on it five minutes before. He wasn't looking at the roosters; he was looking at me, with the shadow of a smile hovering about his full lips, his black eyes cold as steel. I got the message: these were his chickens and he wanted to know what I was doing within pecking distance of them.

It was no time for the *no comprendo* bit. I nodded enthusiastically and echoed, *"Magnificos, si!"* He relaxed into a smile that looked like it would go well with the distribution of largesse to the peasants at Christmas. *"Son muy fuertes,"* he said. *"Muy bellicosos."* He made some karate-type gestures, and the light dawned. These were fighting cocks. I'd seen a cockfight just once, on a civil-rights-type trip to one of the L.A. barrios, and the memory still gave me the shivers. Those beauties were killers, with talons sharp enough to slit a throat before you could say *"Viva la Raza."* No wonder they strutted and raked the floor of their cages so imperiously. I saw before me the equivalent of a corral-full of fighting bulls.

"Magnificos," I said again, thus exhausting all my relevant vocabulary. It was enough to trigger the big man off into a long spiel in Spanish, pointing to one rooster, then another, no doubt explaining why this one was the Muhamed Ali of the lot while that one had the style of Sugar Ray. Most of it went past me uncomprehended, but I nodded and smiled in companionable admiration, and that seemed to be enough for him. Finally he wound up his speech, said goodbye to me with a little bow, and moved off around the cages toward the ladder to the main deck.

I turned the other way, intending to go back to my cabin to pick up some cigarettes. As I threaded my way through the barrels of *alcaparras* I was surprised to see that Dr. Jekyll was still there. He stared at me deliberately as I passed. The stare felt like a fist to the solar plexus, hard and threatening. Apparently the switch to Mr. Hyde was in progress.

Why he should be giving me the eye that said, "Your ass is up for grabs," I didn't know. The only thing that had happened since he was beaming at me and offering to shower me with Chiclets was my talk with the rich rooster raiser. I realized that from his vantage point, it would have looked like an animated and friendly conversation. But why should that get Jekyll-Hyde uptight?

For the first time, I began regretting my ignorance of Spanish. If I could ask this dude straight out what his beef was, I might be able to dispel some misunderstanding. As it was, locked in my *no comprendo* box, there was nothing to do but ignore him. I walked past him and climbed up the ladder, hoping the whole thing would blow over and he would lapse back into character as the sunny, boyish children's entertainer I'd first met.

When I got to my cabin, Raoul was up and dressed, with coffee and rolls on a tray beside him. He waved silently and went on eating. I found the dining room and did in my portion of the same, and then went for a walk around the promenade deck. The deck-chair contingent was already out in force The middle-aged couple from my table waved to me and I waved back, not breaking my stride.

Then I saw a face that made me stop abruptly—the white-skinned, blue-eyed beauty I'd eavesdropped on the night before, my Dulcinea. She was wearing slacks and a knitted top that showed off a figure as good as that of the dame I called Carmen, if a little less lush. She was talking animatedly to an older woman in the deck chair beside her, a tall bulky figure encased in a green tweed cape with a straw sunhat tied on with a scarf. Beneath the sunhat I saw a craggy sort of face, with a hawklike nose and high cheekbones, the skin weathered but not wrinkled, the eyebrows imperious. In spite of the marked contrast with Dulcinea's delicate features, there was the same look of the aristocrat about her, a look which said she knew who she was and didn't give a damn what anyone else thought.

To my delight, I saw there was an empty deck chair beside the older woman. I sat down beside her, nodded pleasantly, and broke my "*no comprendo*" rule for the second time that morning. "*Buenos dias,*" I said to both women, not knowing how I'd handle the reply, but intrepid enough for anything.

The response was startling. My quarry, the blue-eyed girl, turned two shades paler, ducked her head abruptly to the older woman and murmured something, jumped to her feet and raced off around the deck. I hadn't expected to be welcomed with open arms and kisses, but wasn't she carrying girlish caution to an extreme? Stunned with disappointment, I stared after her, too dazed to make even a pretense of polite conversation with the woman in the tweed cape. However, she suddenly jerked my attention from the fleeing paragon by saying in English, "Off like a startled fawn, she was. Now what would a harmless-looking lad like yourself have done to put such a fear on her?"

"I don't know," I said miserably. "Maybe it's my face. It never seems to do much for me in the way of public relations."

"Public relations, is it? It strikes me your intentions were more along the line of private relations." There was a glint in her eye, whether of moral outrage or humor it was hard to tell.

28

"You're getting a little personal," I said.

"Sure, and haven't I the right to? At my time of life, one is allowed to be outrageous. I've been looking forward to the chance for years."

I thought she was doing pretty well at it, but I didn't say so. Instead I said politely, "Are you enjoying the trip?"

"Indeed I am. It's a pleasure to have the deck rolling under my feet again. Reminds me of the time in '21 I was sent to New York on an arms buying trip for the *Clan na Gael*."

"You're Irish?" I asked, rather unnecessarily, considering her accent.

"To the core. Though the last few years, with the old bronchitis so bad, I've had to spend most of my time in Spain."

"Than which there are worse fates," I suggested.

"Ah, that's better," she said, beamingly. "You're beginning to talk like a human being instead of a Yank."

"I *am* a Yank," I said hotly. During my years in England I had developed a strong allergic reaction to patronizing remarks about my nationality.

"There's no need to ruffle your feathers, lad. I was only joking. But if you're a Yank, the betting is good there's some bit of Irish in you. What would your name be, I wonder?"

Suddenly I realized what was happening. Under the shock of hearing someone speak English, I was letting my resolution about solitude go down the drain. I was getting involved. I was moving from audience to stage. I was imperilling my Grand Plan for finding myself. I must put a stop to this. I grabbed for a defending phrase. "*No comprendo*," I said.

"*Entonces, como se llama, si quiere hablar espanol*," she shot back. "And that's a hell of a way to treat a friendly inquiry from someone who may well turn out to be a relative of yours."

I saw her point. It *had* been a gauche thing to say. "A relative?" I murmured weakly. "How do you figure that?"

"Quit stalling, as they used to say in those Yank films," said my interrogator, "and do me the kindness of telling me your name."

I surrendered. "Brian Singdahlsen," I said.

"Ah! Brian!" she said, with a beatific expression. "Wasn't I right, then. You've the name of the greatest of the High Kings of Ireland, Brian Boru."

"My mother was Irish," I said. "But she never made a big thing of it. My father's family was Norwegian."

"It all comes down to the same thing, of course." I looked at her questioningly. "The Scandinavian pirates were in and out of Ireland for centuries, pillaging our coasts and plundering our women. Left many a live souvenir, as was only natural. Singdahlsen, you say. Now wouldn't that be some relation to our famous writer, John Millington Synge?"

"It would be nice to think so," I said fervently.

"So you approve of writers, do you? I thought all Yanks your age did nothing but watch the telly. In fact, one of your compatriots who came banging his guitar through the campground where I live said as much. 'Words don't make it, man.' That's what he said." Her imitation of the standard hippie whine was ludicrous, coming from that stern, hawklike face.

"For me, words are the only things that do make it," I said. "Unfortunately, I'm not making it with the words very well these days."

She deciphered my code instantly. "You're a writer!" she exclaimed. "I should have known. That mournful gaze, that untidy hair, the look of the bard stamped all over you. Just a moment," she breathed, her forehead

30

wrinkling with concentration. "Singdahlsen. Now it comes to me. I read a book of yours a few years back. A grand jest, about a wee man in a grocer's shop it was."

"You've read *Eating*?" I cried.

"Aye, that was its name. *Eating*. A satire my fellow Dubliner, Dean Swift, would have enjoyed."

I was completely won over. A real live reader of one of my books! The thought of Jonathan Swift as fan club president didn't hurt either. I began to burble on uncontrollably, telling her all about my troubles, my current impasse, Peter's advice on a cure, and my doubts about its working. She listened sympathetically, clucking her tongue now and then. Finally, after she murmured some comforting words about it being early days yet and how important it was not to rush things, I came out of my self-absorption long enough to realize I didn't yet know her name.

"I thought you'd never ask," she said in answer to my question. "I'm Kathleen O'Connell, late of Percy Place, Dublin, now of *Camping La Refugia* near Almeria, on the south coast of Spain."

"*Mrs.* O'Connell?" I asked. She didn't have the air of a spinster.

"If you must be technical, yes," she nodded. "But no one except the Archbishop calls me *Mrs*. O'Connell. If you're too intimidated by my extreme age to bring your tongue to call me Kathleen, perhaps we could agree on something cozy like *Aunt* Kathleen. There must be a family relationship somewhere. What was your mother's name, by the way?"

"Isabel Mahon," I said.

She beamed. "Well, there you are, now," she said. "There was a Teigue Mahon from County Galway was my grandfather's sister-in-law's stepson. So you see, it's all in the family."

I saw there was no use arguing the point. "Aunt

Kathleen it is, then," I said. Something she had mentioned earlier popped into my head. "Did I understand you to say you live in a *campground* in Spain?"

"There's no need for that note of alarm in your voice," she replied. "I'm not one of those muscular old ladies who clamber about the mountains with rucksacks and wee nylon tents. I live in comparative splendor in a rented caravan."

The word "caravan" threw me for a minute, and then I remembered how the English use it.

"Oh, a trailer," I said.

"As you will. I believe that *is* what the scruffy guitarist I spoke of called it. My own private name for it is the Taj Mahal. It's gleaming white on the outside and very comfortable inside. Has a gas cooker, a geyser for hot water and a fridge."

"Sounds like the lap of luxury," I said. "How come you're deserting all that splendor for this antiquated vessel?"

"It's my son, Paddy. He's just gone and made me a grandmother—with a little help from his wife, of course—and I'm on my way to view the latest specimen of the O'Connell tribe."

"Your son lives in Mexico?"

"Oh, no. He lives in New York City. He went there as a member of the Irish delegation to the United Nations, and the place seemed to take hold of him."

"It does that to some people."

"Of course, the British press lords exaggerate the sordidness of the place for their own reasons," said Aunt Kathleen. "If half of what you see in the papers were true, I'm sure he couldn't bear it. I suppose, though, falling in love made it seem more attractive. That does tend to unsettle even the most level head. Not that Paddy's judgment is Olympian at the best of times. He's what you might call impulsive. It runs in the family. My dear husband, Fergus, God rest his soul, was the same."

"So Paddy married a New York girl?" I said.

"He did that. She seems to be a charming little thing, to judge from her photos. They appear to be very happy together, despite all this trouble one hears of with the refuse collection and people being coshed in parks. So much so that Paddy's resigned from the Irish delegation and taken a permanent job with the Secretariat."

"If he doesn't watch his step, he'll find he's turned into an American citizen."

"Not bloody likely. Paddy's too cagey for that. He knows which side his bread is buttered on. It's a great advantage in the Secretariat to be a member of a neutral nation. He tells me neutrals are already a scarce commodity and getting scarcer by the minute."

"It's an interesting point. But let's get back to you, my newly adopted aunt. What in the world are you doing on your way to Veracruz if your son's in New York?"

"If you must know, Brian my lad, I have one weakness. I hate to admit it, but the thought of riding in an aereoplane puts the deathly fear on me. I break out in hives at the mention of it. So when I found there was a ship leaving from Cadiz, only a hundred miles or so from my campground, I jumped at the chance. I do think a sea voyage is so relaxing, don't you agree?"

"I still don't understand why *this* sea voyage," I answered. "Do you realize how far Veracruz is from New York?"

"A few hours on the train, I suppose. I'm fond of trains. Not so fond as I am of ships, but. . ."

"A few hours!" I exploded. "It'll take you at least two days to get to El Paso. And I haven't the slightest idea if Amtrak is running any trains in Texas these days. You'll have another two thousand miles to cover somehow after you cross the border."

"As much as that?" said Aunt Kathleen, looking dismayed. "*Ochone*, now I see why Paddy was so irate when I insisted on taking this ship. If you could have seen the blistering letter he wrote me! I had to soothe him by letting him pay my fare and allowing him to stick me into the deep freeze."

I looked at her in bewilderment, not for the last time, as it turned out.

"My own private name for first class passage," said Aunt Kathleen. "You have no idea how stiff and proper they are up there. That's why I creep off to join the tourist class passengers at every opportunity. Keeps my superannuated blood from congealing completely."

"That's why I haven't seen you in the dining room."

"That's right. I dine in stately splendor amid marble halls and crystal chandeliers. I wouldn't be codding you," she continued, having intercepted my look of disbelief. "In the grand old days when this ship was built, they believed in laying it on with a trowel. The epitome of piss-elegance, that's what it is."

"You seem to have made friends down among us peasants very quickly."

"Ah, your mind's still on the pretty colleen from Cadiz I was talking to," she said, smiling roguishly.

"Is that where she's from? I haven't had a chance to talk to her. And from the way she dashed off, it looks as if she wants to keep it that way."

"That *was* strange," agreed Aunt Kathleen, "her scurrying off like that. She didn't strike me as being shy. Very self-possessed, I would have said. Young girls in Spain are becoming very independent-minded these days. Your Elysia isn't mouldering away behind the iron grillwork waiting for a suitable husband. She's in business for herself, owns a dress shop. Very high fashion, I gather. Probably brings in a tidy profit.

Always a good idea for a writer to marry a woman with a little capital, I think. Don't you agree?"

"Slow down, my darling and most recent relative," I cautioned her. "I haven't met the girl yet, and besides, I'm defintely not the marrying kind."

"Now isn't that just the sort of thing all men say," clucked Aunt Kathleen. An amused smile crept over her craggy face. "Do you know the second thing my dear Fergus said to me when the local I.R.A. commandant brought him to my father's house in Rathmines, County Dublin, to hide out? 'We'll be strictly comrades,' he said to me, 'nothing else. In time of war there's no place for romantic nonsense.' "

"A commendable attitude," I said. "How long did it take you to change his mind?"

"Two weeks," said Aunt Kathleen. "We were married in a farmhouse near Tralee, County Kerry, just before he went off to lead an ambush against the Tans. He got himself captured, and I didn't see him again for eighteen months."

"I take it this was back in the Irish Rebellion—sometime in the Twenties, wasn't it?"

"My dear Brian," snorted Aunt Kathleen, scorn giving her voice a sharp edge, "if I agree to call my beautiful caravan by so plebian a term as *trailer*, perhaps you'll do me the kindness of using the term "War of Independence.""

"Of course," I assured her hastily. "My editor told me I'd been living in England too long. It's led to a certain sloppiness in the use of the language."

"Now don't be too hard on yourself," said my new aunt. "To my mind, you use the tongue with a definite flair. I'm very glad we've met. It's a bit of a relief not to be always casting about for the proper Spanish word, though after three winters in Spain, I can usually manage to make myself understood."

"I suppose the girl you were talking to—Elysia, was it?—doesn't speak English?"

"Ah, the one-track male mind," sighed Aunt Kathleen indulgently. "As a matter of fact, she does speak a little. She'd like to learn more, to keep up with American fashion magazines, I gather." Suddenly she sat bolt upright, looking pleased and excited. "My soul from the devil, Brian! You've hit on the great idea!"

"I have?" It was news to me.

"A stroke of genius," she assured me. "Elysia want to learn English. You speak English. So you offer to give her English lessons. She'll be seething with gratitude. From there on, I'm sure you'll be needing no instructions from me."

"A neat scheme," I said, "but it has one drawback. I don't speak any Spanish, so how can I explain what I'm saying to her in English?"

Her face fell. "Wouldn't you know there'd be a catch in it somewhere," she said. "Never mind, Brian. I'm sure there's a way. Let's put it from our minds now, and let the answer work itself out. We've three weeks ahead of us, after all, and the ship's a small one. She can't escape you forever. Now cheer up, lad, and let's have a bit of pre-lunch sherry."

As I came to know Aunt Kathleen better, I learned not to be startled at anything she did or said, but at this stage I was taken unawares. My reply was notably lacking in the renowned Singdahlsen suavity. "Isn't it too early for a drink?" I croaked.

Kathleen O'Connell's eyes were warm but her voice was a mite frosty as she replied, "My dear Brian, as I was wont to tell my good old friend Eamonn De Valera, who at times used to express similar Jansenist ideas, one does not *drink* sherry, one *sips* sherry." She was calmly pulling a bottle from her carpetbag (I swear it was a genuine carpetbag.) Next she extracted two slender stemmed glasses from the same bag. She poured, I meekly accepted. The sherry had that great nutty flavor that only good Spanish sherries have. I decided that letting Aunt Kathleen break into my precious solitude was one of the least disastrous moves I'd made in the last ten months.

A flurry of children passed our chairs, laughing and chattering at the top of their voices. In the center of the group, Dr. Jekyll was giving his famous imitation of Art Linkletter, smile, cute questions, the lot. He was also handing out Chiclets right and left.

"Father Hernandez is certainly God's gift to harrassed parents," said Aunt Kathleen.

"*Father* Hernandez?" I asked blankly.

"Oh, yes. He's a priest, to be sure. The reason he doesn't wear the backward collar or a cassock or some such flummery is because he's a Mexican priest. The Mexican government outlawed the clerical garb some years ago."

"You've met him?" I asked.

"Just casually. He came up to our posh lounge last night to natter about religion with one of the rich old biddies up there."

"He sits at my table in the dining room," I said. "The children all seem to be crazy about him."

"Am I to take it that you're not?" Aunt Kathleen's eagle eyes held a gleam of curiosity.

I hesitated. Despite her apparent flippancy about priestly uniform, Aunt Kathleen probably shared the widespread Irish adulation of the clergy. I didn't feel like shattering any of her illusions by telling her I'd heard this Pied Piper of a priest talking rough and nasty and manhandling our dear Elysia. But I knew I had to provide some reason for the dislike that had evidently crept into my voice when I mentioned him.

"Just a puzzling little incident," I said. "I was down

on the lowest deck looking at some chickens this morning, and the young padre seemed to be giving me a dirty look. Probably my imagination."

"You were inspecting Don Manuel's fighting cocks, were you?"

"Is that the guy's name? Somewhat portly, definitely rich?"

"Fat as a Limerick hog and rich as Onassis," Aunt Kathleen elaborated. "That's Don Manuel Rodriguez Acosta. His principal occupation is raising fighting bulls. The cocks are something of a hobby."

"How do you learn all these things?" I asked admiringly. "We've been on this ship for less than twenty-four hours."

"Don Manuel is at my table," said Aunt Kathleen. "Gives an amazing gastronomic performance, or at least he did last night. I can't believe he could manage to swill so much every single night. There are limits to the elasticity of even the most liberally constructed internal organs."

"I had quite a conversation with him this morning," I told her, "while we were looking at the birds. Or to be more accurate, quite a conversation took place between us. He did most of the talking and I took care of the nodding and smiling."

"Aha!" Aunt Kathleen nodded in satisfaction. "No doubt this colloquy took place within the good father's range of vision?"

"As a matter of fact, yes," I said.

"That explains it, then. Father Hernandez has a great affection for dumb beasts. Positively Franciscan, he is. The sort who goes around buying caged canaries and turning them loose to the freedom of the skies."

"Or the claws of some alley cat," I commented snidely.

"You scoff. I think it's really rather courageous of

him, particularly in a Latin country where bullfighting is a sort of sacred cow. . . .Oh, drat, that was badly put, but you know what I mean.''

"He want to turn the killer bulls loose to the freedom of the city parks?" I asked.

"He belongs to some society that's trying to make bullfighting illegal. They haven't the chance of a snowball in hell, of course, but it does seem rather a pleasant thing for a priest to be spending his time at. In my young days, too many of them got their exercise by chasing young lads and girls who were doing a bit of harmless courting in the bushes.''

I was relieved. Apparently Aunt Kathleen's liking for priests was tinged with some acknowledgment that they might have human shortcomings like the rest of us. But she still hadn't explained this one's switch to the Hyde side of his personality.

"You just said 'That explains it,' " I prompted, "but you haven't explained it to me. The dirty look, I mean.''

"But it's so obvious. The good father feels the same way about fighting cocks as he does about all our other feathered friends. He disapproves highly of their being corrupted into pawns in a blood sport. He was telling Doña Herlinda last night that he'd like to buy the lot and set them free. But of course, he hasn't the money, poor lad.''

"Are you going to tell me why the dirty look?" I asked impatiently.

"You Yanks do go at everything in such a rush," said Aunt Kathleen, gentle reproof in her voice. "Besides, I would have thought you'd the sense to have worked it out for yourself by now. When the good father saw you and Don Manuel talking together like boon companions, he naturally assumed you were another exploiter of the animal kingdom. Naturally, that would prejudice him against you.''

I thought about it a minute. Maybe she was right. I still couldn't completely erase the thought that the stormy conversation I'd overheard the night before had something to do with the whole scene, but I might be wrong. Now I wasn't even absolutely sure that this Father Hernandez had been the man mistreating Elysia. A quick glimpse of the unknown man might have led me to jump to conclusions. After all, this guy was a priest, and Aunt Kathleen appeared to approve of him. Then too, he *had* been friendly enough this morning before I'd met Don Manuel; that part of Aunt Kathleen's theory made sense.

"Maybe I was doing the padre an injustice," I said. "But let me ask you one favor. If Doña Herlinda shows any signs of loosening the old purse strings for this worthy cause, give me fair warning. I want to be some place else when those babies stalk out of their cages. Like about five hundred miles away and wearing a suit of armor. I don't think their mothers ever gave them the word about Saint Francis."

"A sense of self-preservation is a valuable quality," said Aunt Kathleen. "I mean to drop a word in the good father's ear suggesting that yon ferocious fowl might be birds of a different feather from canaries. Eliminate the necessity for first aid. Thought it might be edifying to practice the healing art again. I remember one time in Oughterard, County Galway, when some of the lads got badly cut up while ambushing an armored car. I dispensed disinfectant, bandages and splints with a lavish hand, and they all swore I had the Nightingale touch."

I looked at the craggy, handsome face, the hawklike nose. I couldn't quite see Aunt Kathleen as a ministering angel. Still, she *had* produced the sherry, which was definitely increasing my feeling of well-being.

As if she were reading my mind, Aunt Kathleen chose

that very moment to dive into the carpetbag again. The second glass tasted even better than the first. The sun was shining, the sky was clear, a soft salt breeze provided the only visible action. It was a beautiful day to do nothing. Of course, I had been engaged in that occupation for quite a spell now, but doing nothing on a miserable drizzly London day is not very satisfying. Doing nothing on a passenger liner in good weather is. So my conscience permitted me to sip sherry with Aunt Kathleen until the gong rang for lunch with never a twinge of guilt at my idleness.

It was only as we parted to go our separate ways that the old guilt reasserted itself. I found myself just about to suggest that we meet in the tourist class bar after lunch and continue our conversation, but I had a sudden vision of all those months in Greek waterfront cafes, all that *retsina*. . . No! I would not be the slave of old patterns. Aunt Kathleen was a good companion, and no doubt I could benefit by picking her brain, with its encyclopedic knowledge of the habitats and habits of all the ship's passengers. Still I must not succumb totally to her spell. I must think, strive, muse, meditate; perhaps, God help me, even WRITE. So I said something vague and un-nephew-like, perhaps "See you around" or some qually gauche effusion, and went off to the tourist class dining room determined to be nice to Father Hernandez, even if he happened to be in the Hyde phase of his cycle, and above all, after lunch was out of the way, to get down to work. Or some reasonable facsimile thereof.

CHAPTER 3

As usual, most of my good resolutions dissolved into apathy. I did maintain my benevolent attitude toward Father Hernandez, which was fairly easy, since he was back into his usual sunny mood. The carafes of red wine which the waiter kept replenishing helped me to develop some positively friendly feelings toward him. They didn't do anything very great for my creative process, though. I tried some revision on a half-finished short story I'd brought with me, sitting in the suitably solitudinous area above the bow. I would have preferred to work in my cabin, but Raoul was still immovably established there, and his silent presence made me nervous. Of course, his monopoly of the cabin provided a good excuse for giving up my feeble attempt at work in the minimum time acceptable to my conscience. *Why the hell is the guy clinging to the woodwork like that?* I muttered self-righteously. He certainly wasn't seasick. The food on those trays was gobbled up very efficiently. And unlike my virtuous self, he didn't even try to use his solitude for something constructive. The paperbacks, of which he seemed to have an inexhaustible supply, were obviously crime novels and science fiction.

Carrying my grudge against Raoul carefully, so as not to let it dissolve too soon, I made my way to the tourist class bar and devoted the rest of the afternoon to the appreciation of the produce of the San Miguel brewery. Several jovial fellow-appreciators attempted to talk to me, but I religiously kept up the *no comprendo* bit, sitting at my solitary table and basking in the curious stares of my fellow passengers. Brian Singdahlsen, man of mystery. What scintillating comments on the lives of those around him seethed behind that impassive brow!

This form of self-deception got me through the afternoon. About five o'clock an unexpected diversion appeared to get me off the hook for a little while longer: land! Not, as I thought in a first burst of alcoholic dismay, that the ship had suddenly turned into a jet airliner and we were all set to jump into old Chris' footsteps in the soil of Santo Domingo. This turned out to be one of the Canary Islands, and the port was Tenerife.

There was much hustle and bustle among the passengers. It seemed everyone was happy to risk missing dinner on the ship in order to explore the town. I decided to join them. I thought vaguely of hunting up Aunt Kathleen and inviting her to accompany me, but gave up that project as too time-consuming.

As things turned out, I found her very quickly on shore. Apparently Tenerife was in the throes of a fiesta, though I couldn't make out which saint had thoughtfully provided the excuse for this particular three-day binge. Maybe it was an extension of the fiesta that had been raging when we left Cadiz, something to do with *los Reyes Catolicos*, known to every American schoolchild as Ferdinand and Isabella. The program there had consisted primarily of shaking mops of crepe paper in strangers' faces and laughing uproariously. And drinking, of course. I had done my share of the latter in Cadiz, and was prepared to assume a similar responsibility here.

It had been chilly in Cadiz, but in Tenerife the weather was warm, and there were little impromptu cafes scattered around everywhere on the sidewalks and in parks, amid all the crepe paper streamers and firewords. In one of these I happily spotted Aunt Kathleen, and even more delightedly, Elysia. Crossing my fingers in a surreptitious attempt to ward off the startled fawn reaction, I joined them. Elysia smiled, she looked pleased, she showed no disposition to disappear. Perhaps Aunt Kathleen had been explaining to her that my true nature was far more attractive than the rather mediocre physical package it was wrapped in.

As Aunt Kathleen had told me, Elysia did have a smattering of English, and the sparkle in her blue eys, the charming way she tilted her head and smiled made such otherwise non-stimulating phrases as "Do you like the fiesta?" and "Do you like Spain" seem like brilliant shafts of repartee. I suppose all that *cerveza San Miguel* helped too. We added to our exuberance by sampling one of Aunt Kathleen's favorite tipples, a liqueur with a number for a name. It was called *Quarente y Tres*, Forty Three, which probably represented its percentage of alcohol by volume, though it tasted as smooth as a vanilla sundae. The management threw in a plentiful supply of crisp French-fried sardines as an added bonus, or perhaps as insurance against the insidious effects of the *Quarente y Tres*. Nobody likes *too* much broken glassware, even at a fiesta.

All was merriment and laughter and joyousness and similar good stuff until the usual Singdahlsen *karma* reasserted itself. This time it took the shape of the nervous Valentino type who held down the end of my table in the dining room. He headed straight as an arrow toward Elysia through the collection of cafe tables. He looked more nervous than ever, evidently very worried about something. Totally ignoring Aunt Kathleen and me, he leaned over and murmured something in Elysia's ear. This surprised me, since in the dining room, where I'd been keeping a constant surveillance on her, I'd never seen them so much as look at each other. I was even more surprised to see a look of unmistakable terror replace her charming smile. Then she did the startled fawn bit all over again, though this time she had the class to murmur an apology in Spanish to us both as she picked up her handbag and trotted off up the street at a rapid pace.

Meanwhile, the dark nervous dude had split. I expected to see him join Elysia as she mingled with the crowd promenading on the boulevard, but though I kept her clearly in sight for at least five minutes, he wasn't with her. He must have gone off in a different direction.

Aunt Kathleen was taking it all in with her usual perceptiveness. "Well, at least it would seem that rather oily-looking young man wasn't after stealing your girl from you," she said. I had reached the same conclusion, which cheered me enough that I didn't bother to correct her over-optimistic use of the possessive pronoun.

"She was scared out of her skin," I said. "I wonder why? What could that slimy character have said to her?" For a moment I wondered whether *this* was the guy I'd heard arguing with her in the darkness near the bow. I decided he couldn't be. The man I'd half seen was shorter and his hair had been lighter. Elysia seemed to have a collection of pretty undesirable characters buzzing around her.

"You're right, the lass was trembling like a freshly caught trout," said Aunt Kathleen. "There's some mystery in her life, you can be sure." The thought seemed to inspire her with pleasure rather than concern. She looked positively gleeful as she nibbled immediately on a sardine.

With her usual expertise, she caught my look of disapproval. "You'll be thinking I'm taking an unseemly delight in the woes of a poor young maiden," she said. "I'm not really such a callous old bird. It's just that I love a bit of a mystery. Besides, the situation holds an immensity of promise for the match between the two of you which I've set me heart on."

"Fat chance of a match," I said, "if she's going to keep on practicing for the hundred yard dash every time we meet."

"Don't be so ready to abandon the pursuit, Brian lad. Can't you see your opportunity? She's obviously in some trouble, being as you put it, scared out of her skin. All we've to do is to find out what's terrifying her, and remove the danger. Then you'll find the pathway of true love far less rocky, I'll wager."

"Easily said," I commented, "but where do we start? With my ten words of Spanish, I haven't much chance of persuading her to see me as a trusted confidante."

"I flatter myself my own powers of persuasion may be somewhat more formidable," said Aunt Kathleen. I thought she was probably understating the case, and felt a little relieved.

"A very pleasant and aunt-like idea," I said. "I'd really appreciate it if you could get her to explain all this dashing about. And what the shiny-haired character is doing in her life."

Aunt Kathleen was just about to describe some possible methods of worming her way into Elysia's confidence when we were interrupted by Father Hernandez, bearing down on us preceded by his boyish smile and followed by the usual procession of Chiclet-hungry children. He charmingly requested permission to join us, Aunt Kathleen charmingly assented and he sat down at our table, while the children stood around chewing their Chiclets in silent contemplation of the distin-

46

guished foreign old lady and the undistinguished foreign young man.

The padre and Aunt Kathleen launched into a bantering conversation bits of which she relayed to me in English. The talk seemed to center around his role of dispenser of Chiclets to the juvenile population.

"I'm after telling him the next generation of Mexicans won't need an army. They'll have strong enough jaws from chewing his Chiclets to bite their way through any enemies," she said at one point, at at another, "I'm saying it's a pity the government won't let him wear a cassock; he'd have room for bags full of Chiclets under it, not just pockets full."

Father Hernandez appeared very happy with her teasing. He smiled and laughed and made some snappy retorts of his own, which apparently were not quite scintillating enough to induce Aunt Kathleen to translate them. Carried away by the general bonhomie, I remembered an appropriate Spanish proverb I'd picked up in a waterfront cafe in Marbella from a Spaniard who'd been a waiter in Hoboken. So when Father Hernandez, explaining Aunt Kathleen's latest sally, started to demonstrate with sign language his government's prejudice against cassocks, I came out grandly with "*El habitoi no hace el monje.*" It made quite a hit with both of them. "Ah, you're the deep one, Brian lad," murmured Aunt Kathleen. "True enough, the habit doesn't make the monk. Nor does the pretense of ignorance make a certain Yank the *eejit* he would have us think. Only ten words of Spanish indeed!"

Father Hernandez laughed heartily and nodded his head, launching into a rapid commentary on my wit. I realized I'd blown the *no comprendo* bit so far as he was concerned, which was a pity, because I really *didn't* understand the flood of chatter he was laying on me now.

Seeing my predicament, Aunt Kathleen said, "He wants to know if we have a similar proverb in English. I suppose 'Fine feathers don't make fine birds,' is somewhere near the mark."

"Maybe," I said dubiously, being not too keen on mentioning birds in the presence of this latter-day Saint Francis. "Or how about 'All that glitters is not gold.' "

"I'll give him the both of them," said Aunt Kathleen generously, and rattled away in Spanish. The boyish smile didn't waver, but I suddenly got the feeling there was something very forced about it. Small wonder, the poor guy. Look at the kind of life he led, handing out Chiclets to kids and trading aphorisms with old ladies. A pallid existence indeed. He must have to work pretty hard sometimes to keep that boyish smile afloat. I felt a warm glow of compassion for him. There might be worse roles in life than that of a writer who has forgotten how to write.

Buoyed up by this friendly fellow-feeling, I plied him with *Quarente y Tres*, and entered enthusiastically into a pidgin-Spanish plus sign-language plus pidgin-English type conversation with him. By the time Aunt Kathleen finally suggested we might not be too late to get some dinner aboard the *Virgen,* we were all three in a pretty genial mood.

As it turned out, the ship's chef was a flexible sort of person who wasn't at all put out by a flood of hungry passengers descending on him at eleven at night. I suppose the Tenerife exodus was more or less the same on every voyage. So the good father and I rapidly demolished a series of courses while continuing our elementary and rather primitive conversation.

This seemed to make the "*Grew Bee*" enthusiast with the long hair very uptight. He kept giving me dark looks and muttering under his breath. Since I had now definitely blown my cover, I decided I might as well

48

conciliate him by attempting a little conversation with him as well. I did the bit about exchanging names. His turned out to be Jorge Rivera Orozco, which struck me as probably a stage name designed to snare the international artistic set. I tried to entice from him the meaning of the mysterious phrase *"Grew Bee,"* with which he continued to punctuate his conversation, but had no luck. Nor did I become any clearer about why my sudden spurt of friendship for Father Hernandez bothered him. Maybe he had a beef against the Chiclet company.

I had hoped to see Elysia in the dining room and continued the acquaintance that had begun so promisingly in Tenerife, but there was no sign of her. She'd probably eaten earlier, and was now safely tucked away in her cabin. Feeling somewhat weighted down with food and drink, I decided on a brisk walk about the deck before turning in. I dropped in at my cabin to get a jacket, exchanged ritual waves with the silent Raoul, and made the circuit of the main deck several times. Then I stood leaning on the rail in my favorite spot near the bow, watching the stars which were out in full force tonight.

Afterward I wondered if I had subconsciously noted a slight sound behind me and tensed up a little. I couldn't otherwise account for the speed with which I reacted to the feel of an arm coming around from behind me, compressing my windpipe till I almost blacked out. However it happened, my reflexes were just quick enough to supply the necessary countermoves. I'd learned during sporadic attendance at a karate school in L.A.

I managed to break the stranglehold and bang my assailant to the deck, but while I was getting my wind back after this strenuous bit of action, the guy made it to his feet and split, disappearing behind a bunch of packing crates. He left me a souvenir, though, in addition to the bruises on my neck. Something much more tangible. A nasty-looking switchblade knife, open and ready for action. The fact that it was lying on the deck instead of sticking in my back was some consolation, but not much. The guy had evidently taken my unimpressive physique at face value, not figuring on any resistance from me. Now he realized I was not quite that soft, his own methods might get rougher.

Who in the hell would want to come after poor old inoffensive Singdahlsen with a knife, anyway? Some rabid anti-gringo extremist? A secret literary critic who wanted to protect the world from my horrible style? Some man who had his eye on Elysia and had me figured as the competition? None of those reasons seemed serious enough to instigate the rough-house I'd just been through. I decided there was no point in all this maundering about motives. The thing to do was make it to a safe, well-lighted area and try to get some protection.

The well-lighted area was easy to find; the protection was more difficult. I would have liked to use Aunt Kathleen as an interpreter, but when I looked for her in both the first and tourist class bars, she was nowhere to be seen. I figured she'd gone to bed. I managed to convey my experience to the purser, who then latched on to an officer who I supposed was the first mate. They both looked skeptical, though they did take the knife pretty seriously. I had the feeling they thought the *Quarente y Tres* had affected me to the point of hallucination. They were almost surly about accompanying me with flashlights to the scene of the struggle.

Of course, there was nothing to be seen there, not even a few convenient drops of blood. Our conversation ended unsatisfactorily from my point of view, as they seemed to be more or less patting me on the shoulder and saying, "there, there, go get some sleep and don't worry."

They did carry off the knife with them, though. I hoped it was as illegal a weapon in Spain as it was in our own country, so they'd lock it up somewhere nice and safe. A new thought struck me. I began hoping they hadn't got it into their heads that *I* was the owner of the nasty tool and were plotting to turn me over to the authorities or throw me in the brig.

I must have looked markedly perturbed when I reached my cabin, because Raoul gave me a concerned look instead of the usual airy wave and asked, "*Que pase?*" Grateful for any sign of commiseration, I explained to him, with graphic pantomime, my narrow escape from the briny deep. He was gratifyingly horrified, and broke his silence with a profuse melange of English and Spanish.

"*Es* me," he said pounding his chest. "*Es* me, no *usted*. They out to—*que dice*—getting me. *Enimigos mios, enimigos poiticos. Por* me, no *por usted*!" Here he repeated my pantomime of the clutch on the windpipe. "Bad guys, berry bad guys."

I must have looked incredulous, because he went on to demonstrate with signs that we were roughly the same height and shape, pulling me beside him in front of the mirror as he gestured. He was right about that. We were very similar in build. Somebody could have followed me from our cabin, mistaking me for Raoul. But why?

"*Por que?*" I asked, summoning up two of my ten famous words.

"*Soy revolucionario*," said Raoul. That was clear. "*Partido revolucionario en Hermosia*." That checked out too. Some generals had just engineered a bloody coup in that small Latin American country, with the usual quota of executions and "suicides" among the

51

officials of the defeated government. "*Soy jefe del partido revolucionario,*" he added. I took that to mean he was a big shot in the revolutionary party. "*Soy incognito, pero mis enigmigos* lookee-lookee. *Son cochones - que dice*—peegs, *entiende? Muy peligrosos.*"

He was getting really worked up. I thought he'd probably been reading too many spy stories. He sure didn't look like the Che Guevara type. He looked more like the bank teller in the second cage, the one who's never going to make it to higher echelons. Despite the bit about our physical resemblance, I didn't believe anyone was out to knife him for political reasons. After all, that kind of thing just doesn't happen on respectable ocean liners. At least, not when Singdahlsen is writing the script.

I managed to get Raoul calmed down, acceding to his worried instructions by locking the cabin door securely. I made soothing noises and said, "*manana*" a lot. In fact, I treated him in the same condescending and skeptical way the ship's officers had treated me. It seemed the only course, at the moment. Tomorrow maybe I could get Aunt Kathleen into the act and clarify the situation. The thought didn't do much for my nerves. I figured Raoul and I both were in for a definitely restless night.

Round about dawn, I finally achieved something useful in the way of sleep. I woke late, and found Raoul already munching away on his rolls and coffee. He made concerned noises about how I felt, and I reassured him with another of those ten words while I dressed rapidly and headed for the dining room.

Breakfast was a haphazard event on the *Virgen de Toluca*, with people drifting in and out on their own private schedules. The only other people at my table were Jorge, the aspiring actor, and the tall dark nervous dude who'd mysteriously chased off Elysia in Tenerife.

He still looked tense and nervous. I wondered if maybe he had an ulcer. Then I wondered about him a little more. He looked like a pretty agile type. Could his hands have been playing around with my windpipe the night before? Maybe my guess that somebody was jealous of me because of Elysia wasn't so crazy after all.

Jorge was smiling and saying something was "*Grew Bee.*" By the direction of his gaze, I gathered the something was Carmen, the lush and lavish beauty, who was presiding over her coffee and the usual tableful of admiring males over in the corner. I remembered what a foul mood Jorge had been in the night before, when Father Hernandez and I had been yakking it up. Had I unwittingly offended his Latin pride somehow? He sure had looked pissed off about something. Enough to try to dump me in the ocean, though? I thought not. He seemed too childish and scatterbrained for an effort like that. At any rate, whatever had been bugging him last night had apparently blown over. He was a friendly and garrulous as the first day we'd met. I listened to him absentmindedly, nodding and saying "*Es verdad*?" at regular intervals. As usual, his main topic of conversation was himself. I let my eyes wander around the room. Elysia wasn't there. Maybe she'd already eaten and gone up on deck. She might even be sitting with Aunt Kathleen right now, pouring out the story of her mysterious woes! The thought was a cheering one. I gulped down my coffee quickly and left poor old Jorge hanging in mid-sentence. I was getting mule-headed about Elysia now. I wanted to find out what this startled fawn business was all about. Besides, I welcomed the chance to discuss last night's attack on me with someone who understood English. Particularly someone like Aunt Kathleen who commented so casually and know-ledgeably about ambushes.

I made a rapid circuit of the main deck. Elysia was

nowhere in sight, but Aunt Kathleen was ensconced in a deck chair, her green cape billowing a little in the wind which was vigorously chasing white clouds across a deep blue sky. She waved to me and I quickly settled myself beside her.

" 'Tis a grand day, Brian, wouldn't you say? We've been needing a bit of wind to clear the cobwebs from our brains. I hope you slept well?''

"Not too well, Aunt Kathleen. Attempted murder doesn't exactly encourage sweet dreams.''

"Attempted murder, is it? Do you mean you're writing a thriller? A waste of your satirical talents, if you ask me.''

I was in no mood for another sympathetic discussion of my alleged talents. "I'm not writing anything," I told her. "This was a real life attempt. Or maybe I mean a real death attempt. On me.''

"Brian, lad, your wits are evidently a wee bit addled. Please take pity on an old lady's waning powers of comprehension and explain this whole situation slowly and clearly.''

So I told it to her clearly and slowly, and she listened with appropriate concern. "And you had no chance to see the face of the *gurrier* who throttled you?'' she asked thoughtfully.

"No. It could have been anyone.'' I ran down the list of motives I'd concocted: jealousy over Elysia, some unconscious insult resented by Jorge, a possible violent anti-gringoist. In the bright clear day they all seemed feeble and unlikely reasons. I admitted as much to Aunt Kathleen. "And then there's the most ridiculous of all. My cabin mates thinks someone mistook me for him. Says his political enemies are after him.'' I smiled. Aunt Kathleen did not smile. The hawklike face was deep in concentration. Finally she said, "Political enemies are nothing to scoff at, Brian. When you've seen cousins

54

and brothers killing each other over politics. . . ." She broke off. "But it's the present we must think of. Tell me more about this cabin mate of yours."

"His name is Raoul Alvarez Paredo. He's about my age and build, though his coloring is darker. He stays in our cabin day and night, has his meals brought in on trays. So far as I could understand, he was claiming to be the leader of the left-wing party which just got ousted in Hermosia."

"Was he, now? Anything else you've noticed about him? Anything about his appearance?"

I concentrated. "Oh, yes, there is one little detail. I'm pretty positive he's been wearing a beard and mustache up to a few days ago. The top half of his face is a lot more tanned than his chin and upper lip."

"Do you tell me now!" exclaimed Aunt Kathleen. "That fits perfectly. Have you ever seen a photograph of Antonion Lucho Ruiz?"

"The name sounds familiar, but I can't quite place him," I said.

" 'Tis clear you live in a world all your own, lad. I supose as a creative artist. . ."

"I winced. "Enough of the creative artist bit, Aunt Kathleen. What's your idea about Antonion Lucho Ruiz?"

"He was the second most important man in the deposed government of Hermosia," said Aunt Kathleen, "and following the dashing, if somewhat theatrical Castroite tradition, he sported a magnificent beard and mustache. Now that the reactionary generals have done in President San Martin, there's no doubt your man would be the new chief of the democratic forces."

"You really think this thug, whoever he was, intended to dump Raoul?" I asked.

"Don't look so amazed, Brian. It's standard procedure in revolutions and civil wars. Disorganize the enemy by assassinating their leaders. I remember warning Michael Collins about that. August 21st it was, the very day before he was killed in that ambush in County Cork. But would he listen to me? Not the Big Fellow, not he. Men are so childish, particularly when they're inflamed by politics.''

"Well, this situation doesn't seem very childish to me. I don't like the idea of someone lurking around waiting to knife anybody, whether it's really Raoul he's after or not. The ship's officers were pretty blase about my plight. Maybe if you talked to them in Spanish. . .''

"I was about to suggest that myself, before you told me about your man Raoul. Now of course it's impossible." Her voice was grim and deliberate.

"Why in hell is it impossible?"

"Would you endanger the life of a man fighting for his country's freedom? Think Brian lad. Your Raoul—let's not call him by his true name—is a man on the run. He's trying to keep his identity a secret. Maybe someone has spotted him, but so far as we know, only one person. If we push the ship's officers into a thorough investigation of the attack on you, they're bound to investigate him.''

"And then his cover will be blown," I finished the sentence for her.

"A catchy phrase, Brian. Reminds me of the time Sean Ryan and I were hiding in a haystack near Doonbeg, County Clare. A high wind came up suddenly. . ."

"The phrase is not original with me," I interrupted sullenly, "and if you don't mind, I'm still a little shaken by the thought of people walking the decks with knives. Still, I see your point about not involving Raoul. If he really is this Lucho character."

"Why don't you introduce me to him," suggested

Aunt Kathleen. "Apparently I've been a little more attentive to the newspapers than you. I think I could make sure of his identity."

"But if he's trying to stay anonymous. . ." I protested.

"Never fear, lad. He need have no secrets from Kathleen O'Connell. We have a few mutual friends, members of those left-wing circles you Yanks seem so absurdly terrified of."

I saw there was no stopping her. "All right, let's go down to my cabin. It'll be good to have you as an interpreter, anyway. The poor guy's climbing the walls with frustration because he thinks I'm not getting his message. I'm getting a bit fed up myself with this *no comprendo* act."

Aunt Kathleen heaved herself out of her deck chair and took a firm grip on the ubiquitous carpetbag. "Nonsense, Brian lad. You're doing very well. You understand a great deal of what is said to you."

"I get the general idea," I asserted mournfully. "But every two minutes or so someone comes up with a word that really throws me. Like *Grew Bee*."

"*Grew Bee*? A Spanish word?"

"I guess so. A young actor at my table uses it all the time. This morning he was using it to describe a gorgeous broad."

"By which I assume you mean a desirable female?" asked Aunt Kathleen. I nodded. She thought a minute. Then she snapped her fingers in recognition and said, "Of course. The guitar player. That was the word he used for everything of which he approved. Apparently a very high compliment in your own benighted land."

"It's an English word?"

"American, I think. Perhaps imported to England by the more raffish of our clodlike neighbors across the Irish Channel. I'll give you a clue, Brian." Her eyes were twinkling rogueishly. "In Spanish, the letters "b" and "v" are practically undistinguishable."

The light dawned. "*Groovy*," I moaned. "For Christ's sake! My old brain just isn't equipped for life in the global village." Her eyes lit up. I forestalled another admiring comment on my creative powers. "That's not my phrase either, it's MacLuhan's."

"Oh! A *Canadian*, I believe." A Canadian was clearly one step lower than a Yank in Aunt Kathleen's catalog. "*Whisht*, now, never mind your actor fellow. It's a brave rebel on the run we need to communicate with. On to your cabin, lad. Full steam ahead!"

Actually, my cabin was back toward the stern, but I wasn't about to criticize anyone else's way with words. We descended into the bowels of the *Virgen* and I knocked on the door of my cabin before entering. Raoul looked a little alarmed when he first sighted Aunt Kathleen, but she burst into a rousing speech in Spanish which soon had him smiling with delight. They began trading names, apparently those of the mutual friends Aunt Kathleen had mentioned. Suddenly she checked the flow of conversation long enough to say to me, "Your Raoul is the very man I told you he was. He's heading for Mexico because he has friends there who can protect him while he plans for a new revolution."

"You two sure sound like old school chums at a class reunion," I said.

"Once a revolutionary, always a revolutionary, Brian," said Aunt Kathleen. "It's not age that cools the rebel spirit, but the poison of success."

"One man's feat is another man's poison?" I suggested. The phrase—my own, for once—brought no appreciative glow to Aunt Kathleen's eye. She was back into the name-dropping bit with Raoul. Feeling like a fifth wheel, I silently edged out the door, picking up my clipboard and writing paper from my bunkside table as I went.

This time I didn't try for solitude. I had resolved never to be alone anywhere on that lumbering vessel so long as unidentified people with knives roamed its decks. So I went to the tourst class bar, which was fairly empty at that hour, ordered a lemonade, and began to work on a new idea which had popped into my head during that restless night. This time the writing went better. It might have been the healthy squirts of adrenalin which had been pepping up the Singdahlsen bloodstream during the last twelve hours. Or maybe just that the bar fitted my working habits better than the solitary prow. As I had told Peter, I liked to have a few humans bustling around me, so long as they left me alone. There were several passengers wandering in and out during the two hours I sat there scribbling, but this time, seeing me at work, they didn't attempt camaraderie. I began to understand how people like Sartre managed to write in sidewalk cafés.

There was one passenger who did distract me for a bit—the luscious chick I'd labeled Carmen. Not that she tried to talk to me. She wasy busy enough chatting with her usual entourage, including the husband/boyfriend character. It was just that her neatly tailored pantsuit showed off her classy architecture even better than that clinging dress had. I watched her appreciatively for a good five minutes, but then the Singdahlsen brain began whirring again in a manner I hadn't experienced for five or six months, and I plunged zestfully back into the old C.P.*

By the time the gong rang for lunch, I was in a very cheerful mood. Perhaps my career was about to come

*Singdahlsenese for Creative Process.

up with its second wind! At the table, I abandoned the *no comprendo* bit for good and all, and chatted amiably away in English, Spanish and sign language to all and sundry, exchanging a few "groov*ies*" with Jorge, teaching Father Hernandez a few words of English, letting the kids teach me a few words of Spanish. I finished the meal with a newly enlarged vocabulary of fifteen Spanish words and a pleasant buzz from the red wine. I even stopped worrying about lurking knife carriers. The only cloud on my personal horizon was the fact that Elysia, who was again sitting at the next table, appeared to be completely unaware of my existence. Ah, well, Aunt Kathleen probably had been so busy talking to her revolutionary buddy that she hadn't gotten around to charming Elysia into a more accessible frame of mind. After all, this was only the third day of our voyage. Plenty of time left before she'd have a chance to disappear from my life forever.

My sunny mood continued through an afternoon spent dozing in a deck chair and playing a few games of ping pong with Jorge. It's a tricky game on board ship, I can tell you. The ball seems to develop a mind of its own, ignoring Newton's laws completely. After Jorge had beaten me three games to two, we retired to the tourist bar for a couple of San Miguels. That's when I found out what had been bugging him the night before, when he scowled his way through supper. As we sipped the good Spanish beer, we got the sign-and-pidgin exchange going efficiently enough for him to explain that he was a fierce enemy of the Church, considering it the oppressor of the poor and the chief bulwark of the Establishment. He'd learned *that* word from the same dictionary as "Grew Bee", apparently, because it came out "*Eee-tab-miento*." Hence his dislike of Father Hernandez and his disapproval of my sudden demonstration of geniality toward the priest.

It seemed to me pretty unfiar to blame all the sins of our current social system on a mild and inoffensive Chiclet dispenser, but I knew from experience there was no point in trying to bridge the generation gap. Jorge was ready to humor me as a fellow artist, but the fact remained that I *was* Over Thirty. Consoling myself with the thought that I shared that evil condition with people like Ginsberg and Leary, I listened to his diatribe in tolerant silence, which was all he really wanted. It had been clear from the beginning of our acquaintance that the sound of his own voice was sweeter to his ears than anyone else's raspy vocal efforts.

After dinner, I discovered there was dancing in progress on the upper deck, where a hi-fi pierced the silence of the warm night with some records apparently purchased around 1953 and played fairly constantly ever since. Everybody seemed to be enjoying the scene, however, even a mod character like Jorge. Over on the sidelines, where the bartenders had set up some table, I saw Aunt Kathleen sitting with a group that included Don Manuel, the luscious Carmen and her possessive male, and Father Hernandez. I was surprised to see the padre there after what Aunt Kathleen had said about his attitude toward the rich animal-corrupter. Then I figured he might be trying the soft-sell approach, gradually appealing to Don Manuel's better nature.

I was disappointed that Elysia was nowhere to be seen. But the opportunity of a formal introduction to the boat's other star attraction was some compensation. I went over to the table and was promptly invited by my new-found aunt to join the group. I sat down, and she made introductions all round, while a waiter magically caused a glass of *Quarenta y Tres* to appear on the table before me. I learned that the woman I'd called Carmen was actually named Graciela Lopez de Garcia. The hefty character with the mustache was indeed her husband, Victor Garcia Paz by name. (Some day I am going to get a Spanish women's lib type to explain how this family name system works.)

My self-esteem, already at a record-breaking level, rose a few more notches when I discovered that my detection of a show-biz aura around Graciela had a solid basis in fact. The good old Singdahlsen powers of observation were reviving! She turned out to be a singer, apparently pretty famous in her home town of Caracas. She and her hubby were returning there after a successful series of night club appearances in Spain. She was very chummy with Don Manuel, who was making no effort to allow any open space between his paunchy form and her *Grew Bee* curves. Victor didn't seem to mind. I guess he figured Don Manuel didn't have much chance of trespassing on his property. I wondered if he might be making a mistake. Women like Graciela usually have an acute ear for the sweet sounds that money makes. "Rich as Onassis," Aunt Kathleen had called the big man, and tonight he looked even more opulent than the first time we'd met, down among the chickens. He was wearing an expensively tailored white linen suit, and the shoes on his pudgy feet were obviously handmade Italian jobs. A few diamonds sparkled on various knuckles. Graciela was being extra charming to him, I thought, and then felt like a cad when she started being very very charming to me as well. Certainly there was no hint of riches about the Singdahlsen facade. But the smiles and beguiling little maneuvers with the eyelashes she directed my way seemed to be of equal calibre to those Don Manuel had been lapping up so eagerly. I decided she was either a very good actress or that she genuinely liked me, whatever their shapes, sizes, or Dun and Bradstreet ratings.

She was turning some of the charm barrage on Father Hernandez as well, stepping down the voltage a mite in respect for his calling. He responded with good natured amusement, and with great self-restraint refrained from offering her a Chiclet. Apparently even he could see that she was definitely not the sort of broad to whom one offers Chiclets. Champagne, yes, or perhaps mink. Diamonds, if there happened to be some handy. Not Chiclets.

The padre and Don Manuel appeared to be on good terms. There was no feel of tension between them. I figured I was right in guessing that Father Hernandez was relying on a softening-up process to persuade Don Manuel of the error of his ways. He was very attentive to the big man, and laughed merrily at his jokes. Actually the jokes, as Aunt Kathleen translated them to me, were pretty good. Unlike so many rich people, Don Manuel seemed to have a tremendous zest for life. He obviously enjoyed a good time, and he liked others to have a good time too. When I'd tried to pay for my *Quarenta y Tres*, Aunt Kathleen had quietly signalled to me that the drinks were on Don Manuel, and any flourishing of pesetas in a waiterly direction would be regarded as an insult to my host. His own drink was champagne, and he saw it it that the waiter kept the ice bucket in front of Graciela and himself replenished with many bottles of the stuff.

Just as he delivered the punch line of one of his jokes, and the laughter burst out in the group, the lean dark nervous man from my table came up to us, leaned over, and murmured something in Don Manuel's ear. The fat man looked suddenly angry and started to make some obviously derogatory comeback. The Valentino type stopped him by suddenly waggling his fingers warningly across Don Manuel's face and whispering a few more words. I figured the character was a suicidal idiot. I didn't think Don Manuel was the kind of person who liked having fingers waggled in front of him. But all of a sudden his angry look turned to one of curiosity. He rose from the table, murmuring "*Con permiso*," to his guests, and followed the finger-waggler off around the deck. Obviously the guy had been asking him for a private conversation. I wondered what there was about him that made him so adept at causing people to skip off from parties—first Elysia in Tenerife, now Don Manuel. It couldn't be his personality. He had all the charm of a paranoid ostrich.

Anyway, our host had left plenty of champagne and similar good stuff behind him, so his departure didn't materially dampen the spirits of our little group. We were chattering away merrily when Don Manuel returned about ten minutes later. Then the gaiety did lose some of its sparkle, because the big man was looking morose and thoughtful. He let the chatter go on around him with no more of his usual jokes or laughter. Clearly, whatever the nervous dude had tokd him was weighing heavily on his mind. Even Graciela's best efforts to wheedle a smile from him failed. After a short stretch of brooding he rose abruptly, said goodnight to everyone in Spanish, indicating with a gesture that we should all go on drinking and put it on his tab. I wanted to ask Aunt Kathleen if she'd caught any of the interchange between him and Nervous Ned, but felt the question required a little more privacy. Besides, I'd just noticed a delightful fact: Elysia had appeared on the scene. She was looking enchanting in one of those halter top dresses that only girls who don't need bras can wear. She was dancing with my dear old friend Jorge, who I was sure had awarded her the *citation de Grew Bee*. I quickly asked Aunt Kathleen the Spanish phrase for "May I have the next dance?" and headed Elysia-ward.

The phrase came out all right, but it didn't have the intended effect. The sudden look of fright with which I was becoming all to familiar appeared on her face, and she shook her head vigorously, evidently making some gracious Spanish apology for hating my guts. Jorge smiled at me in a condescending way, demonstrating how sorry he was that the lady evidently couldn't bear to be parted from him just now, and the couple moved off across the dance floor. At least this time she didn't disappear entirely from view, but in essence it was the startled fawn routine all over again.

Gloomily wondering if maybe it was time to abandon Elysia and pursue my muse singlemindledly with no time out for blue-eyed black-haired Spanish girls, I left the festivities on the top deck and went down for a solitary walk around the promenade deck. In my chagrin, I'd forgotten all about my resolution not to take any more lonely walks, particularly at night. Suddenly something happened that brought that precaution sharply into focus again.

From ahead of me on the shadowy deck came the unmistakable sounds oif a fist fight, a real battle royal, with no nonsense about sportsmanship or friendly horseplay. I heard the crunch of a fist against bone, assorted grunts and curses, the whack of a body against the deck, and then the sound of running feet. Suddenly a voice I recognized as Don Manuel's was shouting something loud and angry in Spanish. The deck was immediately flooded with light, and a ship's officer with a couple of the crew materialized from nowhere, along with excited passengers in bathrobes and slippers.

Without any conscious thought, I suddenly took off past the excited group in the direction I'd heard the running feet disappear. Judging from his messed up suit and disheveled hair, Don Manuel had obviously been attacked, and the odds were that his attacker was the same guy who'd jumped me the night before. This time he wasn't going to get away. I reached the front section of the promenade deck in record time, and saw a running figure ahead of me. I doubled my speed and caught up with him, and hit him with a flying tackle that brought us both to the deck, grappling and wrestling. I managed to get a good hold on him, and was delighted when a flashlight beam hit us at that point and one of the crewmen grabbed hold of him. One grabbed hold of me too, but so long as the deck-lurker was in custody, I was sure I could talk myself out of that.

I wasn't at all surprised by the face of the guy I'd floored. It was the tall nervous dude, all right. I still didn't know just why he should be out after either me or Raoul, why he should have switched his attentions to Don Manuel (whose build certainly could not be confused with any other passenger's) or what strange connection he had with Elysia. But I felt pretty good about capturing him and putting an end to any further midnight machinations he might have in mind.

My pleasure was short-lived. Don Manuel arrived on the scene, still brushing off his linen jacket which looked very much the worse for wear, and immediately demanded that my quarry be released. Evidently his word was law on this ship, because the nervous dude was immediately dropped like a hot potato. Then he, in turn, explained something about me to the officer, and the gorilla who'd been twisting my arm behind me abruptly let me go and apologized with a sickly smile. I considered that the track star I'd snagged had pretty good manners, considering the way I'd just been roughing him up. But I couldn't understand why Don Manuel had gone to bat for the guy who had apparently just tried to dump him.

Luckily my personal interpreter, Aunt Kathleen, appeared on the scene just then, having picked up the welcome scent of mayhem. I filled her in on my activities of the last ten minutes, and demanded to know what the hell Don Manuel was up to. She translated this into something more ladylike, and the situation eventually became clear.

"Don Manuel says this man, Arturo Urbino, is his secretary. He just hired him tonight, apparently. Arturo was nearby when a third person attacked Don Manuel, and made a daring rescue. He had beaten the villain, who ran off into the darkness, and was trying to catch him when you hove in sight. He understands your natural mistake, in identifying him as the criminal, and is sorry you were inconvenienced, but the real culprit is still at large."

"Due to my getting into the act," I said gloomily.

"Never mind, Brian lad, you did your best. They're saying very nice things about you, *valor* and *machismo* and all that."

"I still think there's something fishy about this Arturo character," I said. "Don Manuel sure didn't greet him like a long lost buddy earlier tonight."

"I'll admit there's something strange about the whole shebang, Brian, but now's not the time to puzzle it out. You're still shaken up and angry. If you'll consider so daring a course as to accompany a lady to her cabin, I'll provide a reviving draught of John Jameson's fifteen-year-old whiskey. All this Spanish treacle and fizzy lemonade is well enough for ordinary occasions, but in moments of crisis, what's required is a drop of the craytur. You'll see that I'm right."

She was right. The smooth golden liquid with the slight smoky taste quickly knitted up my ravelled nerve ends. Aunt Kathleen joined me, of course, and we sipped in companionable silence for a while. Then she said, "That's better, now. The wild look is gone from your eyes, and you're no longer panting like a horse has just won the steeplechase at the Curragh, County Kildare. Now we can discuss this nasty bit of business in a sensible fashion. You still feel there's something awry with your man Arturo?''

"You saw for yourself that Don Manuel looked angry when Arthur first approached him."

"He went off into the night with him, all the same."

"And came back looking worried, remember? Did you hear what he said to the old man to pesuade him?"

"I did not, more's the pity, and me with my ears strained to the snapping point, curious old biddy that I am."

"Maybe he has some hold over Don Manuel. Some secret from his past Don Manuel doesn't want revealed."

"Perhaps you *should* be writing thrillers after all, Brian."

"I know it sounds far-fetched. But there are some very weird things going on aboard this ship. It could even be that Arturo was really the man who jumped Don Manuel, and Don Manuel is protecting him to keep him from talking."

She simply raised her eyebrows skeptically.

"Come on, Aunt Kathleen. I can see you're not buying my theories about Arturo. Why not? Isn't it possible Don Manuel has some guilty secrets in his past?"

"To be sure, Brian, that's well within the realm of possibility. I gather that although he's a rich man now, when he arrived in Mexico years ago he had very little money. No one's quite sure how he managed to build up his fortune."

"Do you know where he came from originally?"

"That's vague too. Some of my informants say Argentina, some say Spain."

"I suppose there's no way of telling where the slick-haired Arturo comes from?"

"His accent sounds Spanish. Andalusian, to be specific. Somewhere from the south of Spain, anyway."

"So there may be a connection."

"Brian lad, I'll be frank with you. I think you're down on this Arturo because of his mysterious relationship with your bride-to-be. Isn't that so?"

"Yes," I admitted. "I already had some idea that he was the guy who jumped me, and thought the attack had something to do with Elysia."

"Actually, since I take a less personal view of him, his story sounds very plausible to me. I believe we should be searching our brains for the identity of the third man on the scene, not indulging in idle speculations just because you don't like the way a man combs his hair."

"Touché," I conceded. "Your turn to guess."

"If you must know, I was wondering a little about Victor Garcia."

"Graciela's husband? How does he come into the act?"

"It struck me that Don Manuel and Graciela were enjoying each other's company a little too obviously."

"Victor didn't seem to mind."

"Ah, Brian, an open-faced innocent like yourself wouldn't understand the Latin male. While they're charming you with the friendliest of smiles, they may be inwardly bubbling with jealously, like poteen brewing in a mountainside still. Besides, he wasn't with us on the top deck when Don Manuel was attacked. He said he as going to the loo, but who's to know? He hadn't yet come back when Father Hernandez came to tell us about the attack."

"Hmmm," I said. "Maybe. But that would take us back to Square One so far as last night's attack on me is concerned. I hadn't met Graciela until tonight."

"Perhaps the two attacks weren't connected," she said. I looked skeptical. "At any rate," she persisted doggedly, "You must admit Victor's name should stay on our list of suspects until further notice."

"All right," I said. "Maybe we could manage to talk to Graciela tomorrow. If she suspects he had a hand in the fracas, we may be able to pick up some reaction from her, nervousness maybe, anxiety. . ."

Aunt Kathleen sighed. "You think that one would give anything away? Yon lassie's such a consummate actress she'd have you believing the moon is made of green cheese and sending the waiter out for a slice of it."

"To me she seems a pretty square shooter," I said.

"Westerns you're concocting now, is it?" said aunt Kathleen frostily.

I dropped that line of talk hastily. Clearly Aunt Kathleen and I used different gauges for assessing personality. "Can you think of anyone else on board who might e an enemy of Don Manuel's?" I asked.

Her face clouded over. "Well, now," she said, "I'd hate to make any hasty judgments. 'Tis a sin against charity."

"You've just been making hasty judgments right and left," I said. "Why stop now?"

She considered for a moment. "Ah, yes, Brian. I mustn't let personal feelings or political sympathies muddy up the flow of my thoughts."

"Political sympathies?" I asked, sensing where she was heading.

"Your man Raoul," said Aunt Kathleen. "In the course of our conversation this morning, he happened to mention that Don Manuel has important business interests in Hermosia. 'Bloated capitalist' was the term he used, as I recall. He believes the man donated large sums of money to the generals who overthrew the democratic governments."

"For Christ sake!" I exclaimed. "That's a motive and a half for you. And look," I added excitedly, "it would account for the attack on me too. He might have staged a fake attack on me just to suggest that an indiscriminate killer was aboard. Then Don Manuel would seem to be just another in a string of victims, not the prime target.''

Aunt Kathleen looked grave. "There's much in what you're saying, Brian. But, personal sympathies apart, I can't believe the man we call Raoul would take such a risk, being a man on the run as he is. Though I do remember,'' she continued thoughtfully, ''the time Liam Powers sneaked into the Gresham Hotel and executed a British officer, even though the Tans had his photo and a promise of fifty pounds reward plastered the length and breadth of Dublin City.''

"So you do agree Raoul's number one on our Hit Parade?''

"I don't know, Brian. I don't know. Let's sleep on the whole problem, and attack it freshly in the morning.''

"Just so long as no one attacks *me* freshly tonight,'' I said gloomily.

"Courage, man, courage. I've a feeling in my bones there's only one performance per night of this little drama. So the curtain's already rung down for this evening. Mind you, it might be wise to go down the inner stairways to your cabin, keeping well away from awkward spots like the ship's railing.''

"Good advice, madame commandant,'' I said. "And thanks for the Jameson Experience.'' We'll talk some more tomorrow.''

She game me a conspiratorial wink as I left. There were lots of shadows on the inside stairways, but nobody jumped me. Raoul was already asleep in our cabin. I lay propped up in my bunk for a good ten minutes, smoking a *Bisonte* and staring at him speculatively. Then I said the hell with it all, and turned out the light.

CHAPTER 4

As it happened, the first woman I conversed with the next day was not Aunt Kathleen. It was Graciela. I was doing my usual afterbreakast tour of the promenade deck, and saw her stretched out sinuously in a deck chair, wearing yet another well-contoured pantsuit, with a yellow chiffon scarf tied around her head to keep all that billowing black beauty in place. She beckoned me to sit beside her. Victor was nowhere in sight. I hesitated, wondering if he was due back from the loo at any minute, then reproached myself for conduct unbecoming a Singdahlsen and sat down. After all, Aunt Kathleen had said I'd been awarded the "*machismo*" label. I had to live up to it.

Graciela was very, very friendly. She'd evidently heard all about last night's fracas. She inquired with sign language and a few English words if I was injured. I assured her I was reasonably intact. She ten launched into an admiring assessment of my looks and talents. Seems she'd heard from Aunt Kathleen I was an *autore famoso*. I smiled modestly. She exclaimed about how blue my eyes were, and with appropriate manual accompaniment, how soft and fine my hair. She admiringly traced the shape of my nose with a delicate forefinger. Before she could get going on other parts of my anatomy, I thought I'd better put the conversation on a less inflammatory basis.

"*Su esposo, Señor* Victor," I asked. *"No esta acqui?"*

She gave a little shake of her head and snap of her fingers that said she didn't know where Victor was and didn't much care, and started on the bit about how strong my biceps were, again complete with gestures. I felt still more apprehensive, but at the same time, I didn't feel like rushing away. She certainly had a choice collection of secondary feminine characteristics, and besides, I was curious about why she was singling me out as the target for this morning. I decided on bluntness, hoping my Spanish was adequate for the tast.

"Señora," I said, *"me gusta mucho* all this." I pantomined her gentle prodding of my anatomy. *"Pero por que me? No soy sombre magnifico."*

She tried to assure me that I was indeed a magnificent specimen of manhood. "You berry nice," she continued. "Me be berry nice to you."

That was what I was worried about. "No! No!" I said, as forbiddingly as I could, under the circumstances. *"Noche ayer* you berry nice to Don Manuel. Someone go *boom boom* to Don Manuel." Here I threw in my standard pantomine of Muhammed Ali. "Maybe *su esposo* Victor? *Me no gusta* someone go *boom boom* to me."

It was a pretty tangled web, linguistically speaking, but apparently she could dig the pattern.

"No!" she said. "Boom boom is *no* because Graciela. Don Manuel *es mi amigo bueno, muchos anos. Mi compadre, entiende?"*

I gathered she was telling me Don Manuel was her godfather. It seemed an unlikely relationship, but I was hardly an expert on Latin American social life. *"Compadre, si,"* I replied. "Boyfriend, no?"

She beamed brightly at this evidence of clear communication. "Boyee fran, no!" she agreed emphatically. "*Don Manuel tiene muchos enemigos,*" she went on. "*Hombres malos.*"

"Bad guys," I translated, with the usual Singdahlsen gift for a phrase.

She beamed again. "*Si,* bad guys. You no bad guy. You good guy. You *amigo de* Don Manuel. Go *boom boom noche ayer* to *ese* Arturo, *el hombre malo,* Arturo."

"You think Arturo's one of the bad guys? Por que?"

"*No se. Mi corazon lo dice.*" She put her hand over her heart. I gathered her dislike for Arturo was just as irrational as mine. Well, we had something in common, then. But I still didn't understand why she had selected me as her target for today. I tried again. "*Pero, por que* you so berry berry nice to me?"

"Ah!" She smiled enticingly again and moved closer, stroking my cheek and breaking into a rapid flood of Spanish, in which I caught only the occasionaly mention of Don Manuel, Arturo, and *boom boom.*

At this strategic moment, who should come strolling past our chairs but Aunt Kathleen. An interpreter! I'd never needed one more. Unfortunately, she was accompanied by Elysia, whom I found delightful to see at almost any time, the single exception being this moment at which the luscious Graciela was stroking my cheek coaxingly and murmuring intimately into my right ear.

There was nothing to do but brazen it through. "Good morning, Aunt Kathleen. *Buenos diaz*, Elysia," I cried gaily, attempting at the same time to disentangle myself a little. "Just the people I was hoping to see. Won't you join us?"

Aunt Kathleen must have heard the desperation in my voice, for she accepted by invitation at once, with no arch remarks about "Three's a crowd." She even tried, bless her, to get Elysia to join us, but nobody was surprised when the blue-eyed love of my life declined graciously and moved on around the deck.

"Well, Brian, you're having some luck in one direction at least," Aunt Kathleen said with a roguish gleam in her eye, as she settled herself in the chair to the left of me.

"I'm not at all sure what kind of luck it is," I told her. "Graciela seems somewhat overdemonstrative this morning. I get the feeling she has a special purpose in mind. But my Spanish isn't good enough to find out what she wants."

"You'd hardly need to speak Spanish to know what that one has in mind," replied Aunt Kathleen with a lewd look which sat oddly on that craggy face. "It's the one form of communication that's truly international, I'd be thinking."

"Please, Aunt Kathleen, help me out of this jam. I really don't think she's after my beautiful body. It seems to have something to do with Don Manuel and Arturo. I'd really appreciate a little help with the translation bit."

Apparently my genuine panic showed through, because her attitude changed immediately, and she began questioning Graciela matter-of-factly in Spanish. Graciela responded eagerly, with many gestures in my direction. Aunt Kathleen nodded sagely from time to time. Finally she turned to me.

"You're right, Brian. Apparently it isn't your charm as a sexual object that concerns her, but your muscular prowess. She's heard about the donnybrook last night, and the way you laid Arturo low. She wants to enlist you as a bodyguard for Don Manuel, who I gather is an old friend of her family. She's very fond of him in a daughterly way."

"Muscular prowess!" I snorted. "I've got about as

much muscular prowess as a baby starfish. Some days my hand starts aching after five minutes of holding a pen.''

''Oh, I don't know about that,'' said Aunt Kathleen. ''You've given a good account of yourself thus far. First foiling the man who attacked you, and then capturing Arturo. Even though he did turn out to be the wrong man.''

''Graciela doesn't think he was the wrong man. She agrees with me that he's one of the bad guys.''

Aunt Kathleen turned to Graciela and asked her about that. Graciela produced what sounded like a torrent of denunciation, complete with the old hand-to-heart gesture. Aunt Kathleen looked unimpressed.

''Hmmph. She doesn't seem to have any more solid reasons to dislike him than you do, Brian. But if you want to take on the job of protecting Don Manuel against him . . .''

''I don't want to be anybody's bodyguard,'' I mourned plaintively. ''I just want to lead a quiet life and get on with my writing. I particularly don't want to get involved with Don Manual and Arturo. Arturo's taken to following his new employer all over the place. I met him with Don Manuel when I went down to say hello to the fighting cocks this morning.''

''Yes, he does seem to be clinging to the fat man like a leech,'' said Aunt Kathleen. ''He eats at our table in the first class dining room now. Not much of a conversationalist, I must say. But certainly very attentive to Don Manuel.''

''So he's found himself a meal ticket,'' I said. ''Whatever the reasons Don Manuel has for taking Arturo under his wing, they're none of my business. Would you please explain that to Graciela, so she can go recruit somebody else? I'd like, if possible, to finish this trip with what my passport describes as 'no visible scars or other identifying marks.' "

Aunt Kathleen started to explain, and apparently was successful enough to set Graciela pouting disappointedly. She had a pretty pout. By this time, she was desisting from further body contact, a fact for which I felt immensely grateful when I saw the bulky form of Victor Garcia coming toward us. Wondering idly why she didn't get her husand to do her godfather-watching for her, I heaved a sigh of relief. He greeted us amiably, said something to Graciela, and she rose to join him. As the handsome couple moved away from us around the deck, Graciela turned and blew me a playful kiss.

"Are you sure you really got your message across to her?" I asked Aunt Kathleen worriedly.

"I'm sure of it, Brian lad. She knows now you're out of the running so far as bodyguard service is concerned. Of course, that doesn't mean she'll not continue to try her charms on you. To a woman like that, seduction comes as naturally as breathing."

"I wish she had been a little less natural when Elysia came along," I said gloomily.

"You never know, lad, you never know. The fact you've found consolation elsewhere may intrigue Elysia. Young woman can be contrary creatures, as I'd have thought you'd know by now."

"Have you managed to discover anything about why Elysia seems so frightened?" I said.

"I haven't had the chance. I've been to concerned about this nasty habit someone aboard seems to have developed of trying to cut down the passenger list by rather abrupt means."

"Oh, that," I said, realizing with surprise that my worry about Graciela's amorous agressiveness had made attempted murder pale into insignificance. "Yes, it would be nice to know mayhem won't be on the program every night. Have you heard anything more about that fracas with Don Manuel?''

"My cabin steward was very informative. He tells me the ship's officers are taking the attack on Don Manuel very seriously indeed. They've organized a protective patrol, concentrated on guarding Don Manuel, but also keeping all the ship's danger spots under surveillance. So I don't think Graciela really needs to worry about her friend's safety.''

"Pity they didn't take the attack on my as seriously,'' I said bitterly.

"Ah, but we're agreed official curiosity about that would have endangered the man we call Raoul. I've talked to him this morning in your cabin, by the way. I asked him straight out if it was he who tried to give Don Manuel the old heave-ho, and he assured me he hadn't. Said that sort of prank was no way to make a revolution, and might well be suicidal to himself.''

"You believe him?''

"Indeed I do, Brian. Your man Raoul's no childish hothead like young Conor Walsh who almost got us all killed while we were hiding out in a barn on the french estate in County Roscommon. There we were, with two rifles among the six of us, and Conor must go take a shot at the lord of the manor. Luckily he missed, and Lord French was a secret sympathizer with our cause, else we'd have had the constabulary of three counties down on us. No, Brian, this man's a serious revolutionary, whose mind at the moment is on organizing and procuring arms, not on killing for spite or sport.''

"I'll admit you're more of an expert on revolutionaries than I am,'' I said. "And I'll admit also that Raoul doesn't look as if he could step on a water-beetle without fainting, much less try to kill anyone. But it still sounds as if he had the best motive.''

78

Just then the high-pitched clamor of little voices heralded the approach of Father Hernandez, unloading Chiclets from the pockets of his sports jacket in his usual style. I wondered where he got his supply. Maybe some devout Chiclet manufacturer in Spain had given him a trunkful in lieu of cash. He sure was setting up a powerful conditioned reflex in those kids. Henceforth, I was sure they would need no urging from parents or teachers to comply with their religious duties. The mere mention of a priest would send them dashing off to church, visions of Chiclets dancing in their heads. Maybe a more effective method of spreading the faith then the swords of the *conquistadores*. At least, a less bloody one. Being a great believer in the avoidance of blood-shed in all circumstances, I found myself feeling very well disposed toward the good father.

He took the chair on the other side of Aunt Kathleen, waved his juvenile flock off to their own pursuits, and launched into the day's big topic of conversation—the attack on Don Manuel. I was pleased to find, via Aunt Kathleen's translation, that he too felt there was something suspicious about Arturo. He had picked up on Don Manuel's initial hostility to the dark-haired intruder, and found it as strange as I did that Don Manuel should suddenly become so cordial toward him as to enlist him as a secretary.

Aunt Kathleen countered with her theory about the possible jealousy of Graciela's husband. Father Hernandez appeared to be impressed by her suggestion. Neither of us mentioned Raoul. So far as we knew, Father Hernandez was unaware of his presence aboard. I knew that a lot of priests nowadays had revolutionary sympathies—witness our own Berrigans, and a bunch of Spanish priests who were currently managing to get themselves into Franco's jails. But so far we'd heard no sentiments from Father Hernandez about freeing the poor from the bondage of the rich—unless you counted his concern about the chickens, and he was soft-pedaling that these days. So there was no point in revealing Raoul's presence to him, even though I, for one still had my cabinmate on the list of suspects.

The discussion meandered along with all of us agreeing that the culprit was pretty safe so long as the evidence remained as scanty as it seemed at present.

"Of course, the rogue may make another attempt, and perhaps give himself away this time," commented Aunt Kathleen cheerfully.

"Attempt on whom?" I asked in alarm. "I assure you he's not going to get a whack at me. Bright lights, plentiful company, and staying away from railings. That's the Singdahlsen program for the rest of the trip."

Father Hernandez said something complicated in Spanish. Aunt Kathleen shook her head and clucked something back at him as if scolding him, then turned to me. "What a state of things, Brian! Even the lighthearted father is feeling a chill in his young bones. He just remarked that thus far the targets have been two of the traditional *bete noires* of the Castroites, one a gringo, the other a capitalist. He says maybe, as a representative of the Church, it's his turn next."

I wondered if Father Hernandez had found out about Raoul despite our caution. Kids are great observers, and he spent a lot of his time talking to kids. Had one of them told him about the funny man who never came out of the gringo's cabin?

Aunt Kathleen may have been thinking the same thing, for she looked as though an unpleasant thought had suddenly occurred to her, and then made an obvious effort to brighten up the scene. She dived into her carpetbag, produced three sherry glasses, and suggested we start the preprandial ritual. The padre and I accepted simultaneously. The sight of the Tio Pepe bottle appeared to drive all thoughts of Chiclets from his mind.

"Here's confusion to scoundrels and a happy and prosperous voyage to all good-hearted folk like ourselves," said Aunt Kathleen, raising her glass. I strongly echoed her sentiments, but a mood of foreboding had settled over me. As I sipped the sherry appreciatively, my thoughts were dark with apprehension. I was sure we had not heard the last of the sinister activities on the dark decks of the *Virgen de Toluca*.

As a matter of fact, we were entering a period so full of peace and goodwill that any pessimism less doughty then the Singdahlsen variety would have gone down for the count. The next eleven days were a halcyon period of floating gently through a watery world under cloudless skies with nothing but gaiety in all heart. All hearts except mine, that is. Unfortunately, I was rash enough to look up that word *halcyon* in my Penguin dictionary. I discovered that, strictly speaking, it refers to the period of calm around the winter solstice. But here we were, sailing into the vernal equinox, the time not of peace but of storms. That had to mean something, didn't it? Despite the unvarying bliss of the weather, I awoke each morning with a sense of foreboding. Was this the day the shit would hit the fan?

But all the storms were in my head. The days continued sunny, the nights lurker-less. Things got totally idyllic when we entered the Caribbean, with the water turning emerald and turquoise and similar pretty shades, the sunrises and sunsets hotting up to a glow that Turner would have approved, the gleam of phosphorescence in the water during the warm nights, the flying fish darting gracefully across our bow. There were no further attacks. Whether that was because the ship's crew were on the watch, or Arturo's constant presence was really a protection to Don Manuel, or because the lurker in the shadows had given up in disgust after having failed twice, the minicrime wave aboard the *Virgen* seemed to have come to an abrupt halt. Life settled down to a soothing routine.

For me, it began each morning with a meeting of the Chicken Fancier's Club down on the lower rear deck. Don Manuel and his shadow, Arturo, were always the first to arrive. Then either Father Hernandez or myself would be the next to appear. Whatever the order of our coming, the four of us were regulars, sometimes augmented by a few of the other passengers, sometimes not. Don Manual would go from cage to cage, talking Spanish babytalk to each of his proteges, sometimes sticking a stubby finger into a cage to nudge a choice morsel of grain toward a rapacious beak. I thought he was taking some dangerous chances, but apparently they regarded him with the same filial feeling that Graciela did, and never attempted to nip the intrusive finger. Father Hernandez would pause in his walk around the deck, closing the breviary from which he had been reading the prayers God had scheduled for today, and peer at each of the birds in turn, probably giving them some sort of silent blessing. I stood a safe distance back and enjoyed the general cacaphony, the strutting and unfurling of tail feathers. Arturo bit his fingernails and looked nervous, directing suspicious looks at everyone except his patron.

Mid-mornings always included a chat with Aunt Kathleen on deck. One day I gave her an especially vivid description of our morning gatherings, and she volunteered to come down and see for herself. Thereafter, she became the fifth regular member of what she insisted on describing, with ersatz innocence, as a clutch of cock watchers. To the observant Sing-dahlsen eye, she appeared to be paying more attention to the behavior of the various males gathered around the cages then to the feathered inhabitants within them. I figured she had her reasons. I was beginning to learn that Aunt Kathleen had a demonic ability to keep lis-thoughts to herself until she judged the time was ripe enough or her listener astute enough to share them.

My afternoons were devoted to writing. The skeleton of a new novel began to take form. Satire again, damn it, but it looked as though this time I might be able to bring it off. Anyway, it was absorbing enough to give me a virtuous glow of contentment, so the evenings spent boozing it up with Aunt Kathleen and sundry others, usually in the tourist class bar, sometimes on the top deck under the stars, left so stain of guilt on the neo-puritan Singdahlsen psyche.

Elysia continued to be impossible, so far as I was concerned. She was a very sociable girl, spent lots of time with Jorge, danced a lot with all the ship's officers, even made friends with Graciela and her entourage. Only to me did she continue to be aloof, elusive and elsewhere. I still felt an undercurrent of unexplained fear in her manner during our occasional brief encounters, but Aunt Kathleen reported no success in digging out the deep dark secret that hypothetically overshadowed her life.

At least she didn't show any more symptoms of that strange relationship with Arturo. He, of course, was spending all his time with Don Manual, and appeared uninterested in anyone else.

Graciela continued to be "berry nice" to me on various occasions, but with far less fervor than she'd shown during her recruiting attempt. Victor appeared genuinely tolerant of these episodes, and I began to relax and enjoy them. Just enough stimulation to keep the old hormones circulating, not enough to get in the way of the C.P. An ideal state of affairs.

So the *Virgen de Toluca* sailed on and on, as though we might float forever through those jewelled seas and velvet nights. So far as I could see, Elysia and I were the only passengers not completely immersed in a langorous state of well-being. She was still scared of something. And I was keeping a wary eye on the sea gulls, which began to appear in ever increasing numbers. I expected that any moment one of them would pull a Chicken Little on us and squawk "The sky if falling!" Only this time it would really fall. You can see from all this why I'll back the genuine Singdahlsen pessimism against anyone else's feeble imitation of same. Besides, the feel of throttling fades slowly, and I still didn't know whose fingers had been trespassing on my windpipe.

As old Chris had discovered some centuries earlier, there *is* land in them thar waters. We hit it where he did—at Santo Domingo. The ship docked there about dawn. The port area didn't look much like my idea of a tropical paradise, but then port areas everywhere look crumby. We'd seen a lot of encouragingly green vegetation on the rest of the island. It came as a pleasant change from all that water. Even the most beautiful oceans—and the Carribean certainly ranks high on that list—can get monotonous.

The Chicken Fancier's Club held its usual session, since it appeared we wouldn't be able to go ashore until about nine a.m. Some of the other passengers were burbling with enthusiasm over the thought of sightseeing, but Don Manuel waved a jeweled hand toward the shore in a gesture of disgust, and gave out with a few sentences in Spanish that were clearly derogatory in tone. Aunt Kathleen explained to me that the big man had made the trip so often that all sightseeing bored him, and that he found Santo Domingo the least attractive of any of the ports on the *Virgen's* itinerary. This didn't deter the enthusiasts. They went on chatting happily about things to see and do. Aunt Kathleen launched into an earnest conversation with Father Hernandez, and received in return a bunch of negative headshakes and embarrassed smiles. Was he going to skip the sight-seeing bit too?

It turned out that wasn't the case. "The good father's acting rather strangely, Brian," said Aunt Kathleen to me. "I was asking him to accompany us on a sightseeing trip, as my guest, that is. I know the Church doesn't give him much in the way of pocket money. But he won't hear of it, says he wants to wander around by himself."

"Maybe he's just embarrassed at having a lady pay the bills," I suggested.

"Nonsense. If that's the case, he's far different from any cleric I've ever met, and I've known them in ten different countries. I've yet to see one pass up the change of free food or drink."

I glanced nervously at the padre, though I was pretty sure he didn't know enough English to detect Aunt Kathleen's blithe anti-clericalism. He had his nose back in his breviary, and was walking around the deck, his lips moving silently as he rattled off the prayers from his littlke black book. As I swung my relieved glance back to the group around the cages, I saw that Arturo too had been watching the young priest, even more nervous-ly than I. What now? Qualms of conscience, maybe? What the hell, there was no use trying to account for any of Arturo's behavior. There were better things to think about. After all those days on the water, I was as eager as any fanatic tourist to take a look at Santo Domingo.

"I guess that leaves the two of us to do the town together," I said to Aunt Kathleen. "Unless you'd like to buddy up with some of your rich friends from First Class?"

"If you don't mind escorting an antiquated old body like myself about the place, I'd find it delightful to be alone with you for a few hours, Brian. 'Tis a bit fatiguing to be chattering away in Spanish all the time.''

We made arrangements to meet on the dock as soon as we got through the immigration formalities. Aunt Kathleen, being one of the small group of passengers in First Class, was there long before me. I found her wandering around a neighboring wharf, looking at an obviously new shipment of dark green jeeps, all discreetly stamped with chaste white letters saying "U.S.A." They were all equipped with the latest in machine gun mounts.

"I see the Yankee imperialists are still up to their old tricks here," said Aunt Kathleen. I was a little surprised myself, as I had thought we'd washed our hands of the place when we called off the Marines. I guess my inability to produce a snappy comeback softened the old rebel's heart, because she said apologetically, "Pay me no mind, Brian lad. I know you're not responsible for everything your government does. Come now, we'll saunter through the town and find some more agreeable sights.''

We didn't find anything all that agreeable. Peter's talk about sidewalk cafes had whetted my appetite for that form of people-watching, but I was disappointed to find they didn't exist in Santo Domingo. There were a lot of impressive palm trees and flowers, but the people didn't look very happy, and they were dressed even more shabbily than the poor people in Spain. Occasionally a Cadillac or Buick would whizz through the narrow streets while its inhabitants peered out from behind their glass shells like beings from another planet. They didn't look very happy either.

We finally settled ourself in a rather pleasant little park, and watched the comings and goings in the ornate buildings which surrounded it on four sides. Aunt Kathleen happily munched away on some fresh coconut we'd bought from a street vendor. Suddenly she sat up very straight and stared at one of the buildings, every sense obviously quivering, like a hunting dog doing the pointing bit. I followed the direction of her stare. She was looking at Father Hernandez, who was slowly walking down the wide steps of one of the buildings, looking at a piece of paper in his hand.

"I guess the good father is doing his solo wandering act," I said.

"But why wander into the public records office, I wonder?" said Aunt Kathleen.

"Who knows? Who cares?" I said. I was about to suggest that we take our collective noses out of the padre's business and concentrate on enjoying the terra firma, when I saw that someone else was extremely interested in the priest's itinerary. As he moved along the street, still absorbed in the piece of paper he carried, I saw Arturo following him at a half block's distance, his eyes clearly directed at the middle of the padre's back.

"Hey!" I said to Aunt Kathleen. "There's Arturo!"

"She spotted him immediately. "You're right, Brian. Something strange is going on, to be sure. It would take some great mysterious motive to pry that one loose from Don Manual. But we're wasting time blathering here. Come, lad, let's join the good father."

I was about to remind her that the good father had very definitely refused the pleasure of our company, but she had me by the arm, practically dragging me toward the street where Father Hernandez was walking, and I saw there was no stopping her. We were both a little breathless when we finally caught up with him. Aunt Kathleen launched into a torrent of Spanish all the same.

As I had anticipated, Father Hernandez looked anything but delighted to see us. He made a few feeble efforts to interrupt Aunt Kathleen's volley, but either his good manners prevailed, or he recognized an unshakable dame when he saw one. He finally nodded his head in agreement and with great effort produced one of his famous boyish smiles. Aunt Kathleen turned to me triumphantly. "Everything's fine, Brian. He'd be happy to buddy up, as you put it, with us." I wondered why the hell *she* was so pleased about the surrender.

Then Father Hernandez started making a long involved speech about something. Aunt Kathleen countered with one of her own. He finally nodded again, though his smile this time was purely mechanical.

"What goes?" I asked her.

"The dear lad says he wants to make a little trip out of town. A sentimental journey, I gather, to see the place his great-grandfather was born. He wanted to go by himself, and join us later, but I persuaded him to let us pay for the taxi and go with him."

"Are you sure he wants company?" I asked doubtfully. "These Latin types are pretty emotional about family memories. Maybe he'd rather be alone with his ghosts."

"Brian, my lad, there's more to this than meets the eye. I feel it in my bones. Not another carping word out of you. It's all settled." She suddenly darted out into the street, waving the hand that wasn't occupied with the carpet bag, and a taxi came to a screeching halt beside us. We all climbed in, Aunt Kathleen eagerly, her two male escorts resignedly. Father Hernandez showed his piece of paper to the driver, while Aunt Kathleen explained to me the reason for his visit to the public records office. He had gone there to dig up the location of the ancestral acres.

In a few minutes we had cleared the dusty streets of downtown Santo Domingo and were racing through some suburbs, past tumbledown shacks dotted with palm trees and pigs. I sneaked a glance out of the back window. I had seen Arturo jump into a taxi as we drove off, and I was reasonably sure that the same taxi had followed us for a number of blocks downtown. Now there was no car in sight behind us. If Arturo had really been shadowing the padre, perhaps he had got held up by traffic at an intersection. Or run out of cab fare.

The houses thinned out, and were were in open country, with lush green vegetation and palm trees on both sides of us. Then we came to some big mansions, surrounded by high concrete walls, painted in brilliant shades of lime, blue, pink and similar tropical colors, above which towered palm trees and tall flowering shrubs. The taxi driver slowed. Was this the padre's destination? His family must have been loaded with bread, at least sometime in the past.

We stopped just beyond the corner of one of the big walls. There was an open space of about two hundred feet before the next big enclosed house. The vacant lot was covered with tangled and matted vegetation. Father Hernandez opened the door of the cab and we all climbed out. He told the driver to wait for us, and we headed off into the shrubbery. It was heavy going at first, but then the vegetation thinned out to low-lying plants that only entangled us up to our ankles instead of our waists. I realized we were walking on sand now, and sure enough, as we came up over a little ridge, there was the sea in front of us, lapping at a narrow little beach.

"Funny this one lot should be abandoned and undeveloped, with those two palaces on either side," I said to Aunt Kathleen. She asked Father Hernandez about it, and then turned back to me. "He says his family sold it when they moved to Mexico. He thinks the man who owns it now bought it for speculation, and is just holding it until prices go up."

From the looks of its capital city, I didn't think the Dominican Republic was due for a sudden burst of prosperity. Still, looks could be deceptive. There *were* those Cadillacs, few but impressive. Anyway it wouldn't matter to the good father. His interest in the place was sentimental, not financial.

The padre was roaming around among the vegetation. Aunt Kathleen, for some weird reason of her own, was dogging his footsteps. I decided that the beach, though nothing like Malibu, was a better place to be than that tangle of weeds. I wandered idly along the shore, picking up a seashell or two as a souvenir. Just as I came opposite the back of the big mansion we'd just passed, a sudden movement caught my eye. The back of this house was open to the sea. The walls that surrounded it on the other three sides were replaced along the back of the house by a tall thick hedge with several wide openings where paths came through it to the beach. Crouched beside the stretch of hedge nearest me was the lean dark figure of Arturo.

So he *had* followed us! He must have kept his distance and had his taxi stop far enough away for us not to see it. Now he was staring steadily at Aunt Kathleen and Father Hernandez. I didn't like the set-up. Suddenly the vacant lot we were exploring seemed very lonely. I wasn't at all sure either of the two mansions was occupied. If Arturo *was* the lurker in the shadows after all, he might be crazy enough to attack one of us in this lonely spot.

But which one of us? Apparently I wasn't the target this time, because even though I was well within his sight range, he was ignoring me completely. I thought of Father Hernandez' suggestion that he might be the next on some fanatic Castroite's list. That uneasy feeling that the sky was about to fall had been in abeyance during my few hours on land. Now it came flooding back. I'd better go warn the padre.

I waded quickly through the underbrush. The priest

90

was standing a little distance from Aunt Kathleen, his eyes fixed on a spot of ground, his lips moving silently. There was a little pile of stones in front of him. Saying a prayer over the remains of a family hearth, I thought. Not wanting to interrupt him, I said softly to Aunt Kathleen, "Don't look now, but Arturo's here. Sneaking around on the terrace next door."

She didn't seem surprised. "Ah, well, Brian, it's no business of ours where the poor daft soul chooses to wander," she said.

"But why is he following Father Hernandez?" I asked. "I don't like the look of it."

"*Whisht*, now, Brian, I won't have you troubling the good father with your unfounded suspicions. He's in a sad enough mood as it is, as you can see from his distressed countenance."

Father Hernandez didn't look distressed to me. He looked more like a man who was calculating how many Chiclets he had left and whether or not he ought to replenish his supply. He had stopped the prayer bit, and was coming toward us with a smile. I still thought I ought to warn him about Arturo, but for some reason Aunt Kathleen didn't want me to. I knew she'd seen Arturo shadowing the priest. Her shrugging off his presence here made no sense. I didn't know what her little game was, why she'd been so insistent on tagging along with Father Hernandez and why she was no ignoring Arturo when she'd been so interested in him downtown. Still, it was her game, and until she chose to tell me the rules, I might as well let her play it her way.

I caught enough of the padre's Spanish to realize that he was suggesting we go back to town. That suited me fine. We waded through the shrubbery and back to the waiting taxi. The driver had been taking a little nap, his cap pulled down over his eyes, but he was cheerful enough when we woke him up. He had plenty of reason to be cheerful, because Aunt Kathleen shelled out all the good American dollars he demanded without a murmur when he dropped us off in the little park downtown.

Aunt Kathleen was beaming joyously, as if wandering around in vacant lots was her idea of the world'd greatest entertainment. I suggested we might as well head back for the ship, but she wasn't ready for that.

"A little liquid refreshment might go well at this point," she said. "Not knowing how the officials of this reactionary republic might feel about alcoholic beverages in public places, I didn't bring my usual supply. If we could just find some nice little pub . . ."

But there were no nice little pubs to be found. All the bars we peered into were clearly for men only, and apparently for non-Yanqui men at that. We finally discovered a down-at-the-heels Chinese restaurant where the proprietor grudgingly supplied us each with a bottle of Schlitz at a dollar apiece. Gloomily, I watched two Dominican policemen sitting at the lunch counter. They had bought one cupcake and were dividing it between them. The whole scene was getting more and more unlike my idea of a tropical paradise. I hoped Puerto Rico would turn out better. Even though I'm not one of those Americans whose heart leaps up when he beholds a Hilton on the shore, the travel posters I'd seen promised something a little more exotic than this hot, dull burg. I should have taken Don Manuel's advice and stayed out of it.

Apparently the mundane atmosphere of the Chinese restaurant had dampened even Aunt Kathleen's exuberant spirits. She was willing enough to fall in with my back-to-the-boat proposal, though she did insist on walking. To absorb the foreign atmosphere, she said. I said I'd absorbed enough already.

"But Brian, lad, think of your writing. This is all grist

for the mill. You can use it as a scene in a novel some day."

I hate people who tell me what I should write, and I usually let them know it loud and clear. But I didn't want to use strong language to such a nice old lady, especially not in the presence of Father Hernandez. So I went along with her program, and we all walked slowly back to the ship, with Father Hernandez chatting away amiably. Apparently no family ghosts were troubling him.

He detached himself quickly enough when we got back to the ship, an hour before she was due to sail. Aunt Kathleen didn't seem to mind. "Now that we've managed to get rid of the good father, why not join me in some nicely-iced San Miguel to take the taste of the soap-and-water concoction that Oriental palmed off on us out of our mouths," she suggested. I was a little shocked at her callous reference to the priest, especially as she'd been the one who insisted on joining him in the first place. Maybe over a San Miguel she'd lower her guard and let me know what she was up to.

"An excellent idea," I said. "My place our yours?"

"A little grandeur would be welcome after that tacky restaurant," she admitted. "Come be my guest in the first class bar."

The first class bar was a round mahogany-panelled room, liberally sprinkled with mirrors and chandeliers. At the moment, it held only two other customers: Don Manuel and our sneaky pal, Arturo. The lean young man was talking earnestly in Spanish to the pudgy older one. Don Manuel appeared pleased with what he heard. A broad smile lit up his corpulent face, and he patted Arturo on the back approvingly.

I looked at Aunt Kathleen. She was smiling too, the sort of sly secret smile attributed to canary-eating cats.

"I see the great man's secretary returned before we did," she said. "Apparently he's found much to report to Don Manuel about life in Santo Domingo. A bit strange, don't you think, considering his alleged lack of interest in the place?"

"*You* were the one who made sure Arturo had time to get back before us," I said. "And you know damn well what he had to report, though I don't see why the news that an eccentric Irish lady and two undistinguished young men went exploring in a vacant lot should please Don Manuel so much. For that matter, I don't understand why a certain eccentric Irish lady should get much of a kick out of wandering around among the Dominican shrubbery."

"Brian, you're being waspish," said Aunt Kathleen. "As I told you, there's more here than meets the eye. Apparently Don Manuel and I have similar ideas about Father Hernandez. At any rate, it appears that Arturo's rather clumsy effort at shadowing the priesteen was due to Don Manuel's orders. A very astute man, the genial old tub of lard, even if you don't approve of his choice of minions."

"How about letting me in on the secret?" I said, trying to look humble and appealing. The waiter arrived with our two San Miguels, and Aunt Kathleen took a long satisfying swallow.

"All in good time, Brian, all in good time. I have certain ideas about the good father, but they need further verification before I make them public property."

"Letting me in on your secret isn't exactly like publishing it in the *New York Times*," I said.

"You're mistaken, Brian. I'll admit your open and honest face is one of your great charms, but it's also your greatest weakness, when it comes to keeping a secret. You tell me you sit directly across the table from the good father two or three times a day. If I confided my suspicions to you—unproved suspicions at the moment—you couldn't help giving yourself away."

"Aunt Kathleen, I think you're letting your imagination run away with you. Next thing I know, you'll be telling me the Chiclets the padre hands out contain a mysterious delayed-action poison which will have all those kiddies writhing in death agonies three weeks from now."

She didn't smile. She said with an absolutely straight face, "No, not that, Brian. The Chiclets are exactly as advertised." The firm line of the mouth under that hawklike nose told me there was no use trying to pry anything more out of her. We finished our San Miguels in silence, and then went our separate ways.

As you will have gathered, a slight chill had developed in our relationship. A smiliar chill seemed to affect my writing. That afternoon, the C.P. declared a strike of indefinite length. Ideas refused to flow. Words dried up before they reached the tip of my pen. I finally gave up in disgust and went up to the prow to stare gloomily at the water, frothing into white bubbles as the ship plunged through it.

Then I went to my cabin to get a book. Raoul gave me a brilliant smile as I came in, and greeted me effusively. Our relations had been a lot more cordial since his meeting with Aunt Kathleen, but his current gaiety was unprecedented. He looked as though he'd just got the news he'd won both the Spanish and Mexican national lotteries. Of course, my Spanish wasn't up to inquiring the reason for all the sudden sunshine, so I felt more frustrated than ever. Everybody—Don Manuel, Aunt Kathleen, and now Raoul—was going around smiling these unexplained smiles, and I didn't know what the hell they were smiling about.

I sure didn't feel like smiling. Aunt Kathleen might find it a big blast to muscle into the shadowing expedition engineered by Don Manuel and his shady sidekick Arturo. It wasn't my idea of good holiday fun. I had an uneasy feeling that her sort of sightseeing could get us into the kind of king-size hassle which would wipe all the smiles off everybody's face.

CHAPTER 5

The next day someone else started giving with the big smiles. Elysia! What was more to the point, they were clearly directed at me and betrayed an unmistakable intention of encouraging friendly relations between us. I was so amazed I hardly knew how to respond for a few minutes.

The exact location in which this thaw took place was the waiting room of the Mexican consulate in San Juan, Puerto Rico. Since Mexico had no diplomatic relations with Spain, Spanish contingent on the *Virgen,* including temporary residents like Aunt Kathleen and myself, had no opportunity to obtain Mexican visas in Spain. So our first stop, once cleared by the immigration people, was at a tidy little villa tucked away in one of the prettier residential streets of San Juan where the Mexican consul hung out.

There were about ten of us there—Aunt Kathleen, myself, Elysia, Arturo, and six other Spaniards whom none of us knew. I half expected Arturo's presence to put a big black cloud over the whole proceedings, but that didn't happen. He and Elysia ignored each other completely. He sat cracking his knuckles and casting frequent glances at his watch. I figured that being detached from his boss, Don Manuel, for such a protracted time was making him extra nervous.

Elysia showed no signs of nerves. She looked happier than I'd seen her look during the whole voyage. She sat between me and Aunt Kathleen, and kept up a gay conversation, some of it in English, some in Spanish translated by Aunt Kathleen. We talked about the voyage, about her life in Spain, about some American novels (not mine) which she'd read in Spanish translation. I learned that her mother had died several years before, and her father had died very recently. She was getting fed up with her dress shop, and was thinking of trying something new, perhaps in Mexico. I gathered her father had been stinking rich, and his business connections in Mexico would make it easy for her to circumvent Mexico's laws against foreigners invading their job market.

She said she planned to stay in Veracruz for awhile, which made Peter's rosy description of the city suddenly take on a new glow. A technicolor film of me and Elysia sitting in one of those sidewalk cafes surrounded by smogless palm trees began unreeling itself in my head. Meanwhile, I was doing my best with twenty-five words of Spanish to charm her into helpless adoration.

The consul took his time about handing out the visas. I figured the monthly visit of the *Virgen* and her sister ship were the high spots in his official life. I didn't mind his lengthy fiddling with forms; it gave me just that much longer to enjoy this sudden spell of good neighborliness with Elysia. I couldn't shake off the uneasy feeling that once we stepped outside those enchanted portals, she'd revert to the startled fawn routine.

Aunt Kathleen came up with a brilliant suggestion to set my fears at rest. She asked if I still had a U.S. driver's license. Sure enough, my California license was tucked neatly inside my wallet. I saw the light and immediately suggested there must be an Avis or Hertz agency cluttering up the island somewhere, and that we should make use of their facilities to tour the place in our own rented car. While I waited breathlessly, Aunt Kathleen put the proposition to Elysia. She accepted instantly. I was dazzled by her smile and my good luck. She could hardly make any sudden exits while we were speeding along the highways in our own private Chevy.

The consul finally got to us, pored over the forms we'd filled out, and gave us the magic pieces of paper that entitled us to enter Mexico. As we were leaving the consulate, a sudden thought struck me.

"I wonder where Raoul is," I said to Aunt Kathleen. "He's a non-Mexican too. Won't he need a visa?"

Aunt Kathleen smiled tolerantly as she deftly flagged down a cab. "Don't worry about Raoul, lad. No doubt his friends have everything laid on. There are still experts around like our own Tomas Kearney, who once forged an official British order well enough to spring Joe Sweeney from Mountjoy prison."

Feeling like a first grader who's just failed to add two and two, I climbed into the cab and we headed toward Hertz. They were a lot swifter with the paperwork than the consul, and in no time at all we were whizzing out of the crowded and dirty center of San Juan toward those luscious beaches I'd seen on the travel posters.

The beaches lived up to their propaganda. We spent a pleasant few hours strolling along one of them not yet overshadowed by a Hilton, with Elysia wishing she'd remembered to bring her bathing suit. I privately echoed the wish, and publicly suggested that Veracruz might have beaches too. When she answered with a happy smile that she hoped we could enjoy the swimming in Veracruz together, my delight was total and overwhelming. I still couldn't account for the sudden switch in her attitude toward me, but I sure was going to make the most of it while it lasted.

We were due back on the boat at five p.m. The Hertz mad had told us we could leave the car in the customs shed on the dock. But as I turned down the avenue that led toward the boat, Elysia suddenly said something in rapid Spanish. The worried look was back on her face. Oh no, I said to myself, please not the startled fawn bit again!

It turned out she had nearly forgotten some essential purchase she'd intended to make—Aunt Kathleen very coyly refrained from translating what feminine necessity this might be—and wanted to get out downtown and return to the ship by taxi. I tried to persuade her to let me chauffeur her around San Juan, but she refused, politely but firmly. She was smiling again and tilting her head in that charming wway, so I figured the business about shopping was on the level, not just an excuse to cold-shoulder Singdahlsen. I dropped her at a corner, and Aunt Kathleen and I drove back to the dock.

In the course of our beachcombing, Aunt Kathleen had met up with her first daiquiri, and had become an instant enthusiast. She now persuaded me to join her in her further examination of the new art form. We sat in the tourist class bar, from which we had a good view of the returning passengers, while we sipped and chatted.

I noticed Arturo was leaning on the rail near the top of the first class gangplank, anxiously watching the new arrivals. Don Manuel was nowhere in sight. Arturo looked even more worried than he had that morning, and I figured Don Manuel was somewhere ashore and Arturo was suffering the agonies of an abalone who had lost hold of his favorite rock. I couldn't see why he was so worried. San Juan looked like a safe enough place for someone of Don Manuel's heft and shape, by daylight at least. Certainly safer than a ship's deck at night. I was relieved to see Elysia come up the gangplank with several other passengers. We waved, but couldn't catch her eye, and she passed out of sight around the deck. We watched Graciela and her entourage climb back on board with Jorge in their midst. Then came Father Hernandez, who was welcomed by a swoop of Chiclet-hungry children. He didn't disappoint them. By that time it seemed to me that just about everyone was back aboard. I looked at the clock. Five-fifteen. We'd be pushing off soon.

Suddenly Graciele hurried into the bar, all by her luscious self. She looked upset, almost hysterical. She headed straight for us, and burst into a flood of excited Spanish. I caught the name "Don Manuel" repeated several times, but nothing beyond that.

Aunt Kathleen turned to me. "She's worried about Don Manuel, Brian. It seems he hasn't yet returned to the ship. She suspects foul play. I've been advising her to take her troubles to Arturo, since Don Manuel is his employer, but she insists she doesn't trust him. If I understand her rightly, she's implying yon lanky Latin has done the old man in."

Graciela turned her big black eyes on me. "Arturo bad guy," she said, "berry bad guy." I couldn't see what she expected me to do about it. Aunt Kathleen couldn't either, and told Graciela once more that Arturo was the man to handle things. She volunteered to go find Arturo and see how he felt about the situation.

Arturo was no longer by the rail. Moreover, the gangplanks had been pulled up, and as Aunt Kathleen and I, with Graciela following us anxiously, started a tour of the decks in hopes of finding him, the whistle gave two sharp blasts, and the boat began to move. Graciela gave a little moan and went into her hysterical act again.

According to Aunt Kathleen's translation, she was now

insisting that we find Arturo and help her confront him with dark accusations of villainy. Why she chose us for that role, I don't know. Probably because she blamed me for turning down her neat scheme to make me Don Manuel's bodyguard. Or, since I was the only American aboard, maybe she held me responsible for all skulduggery committed on Puerto Rican territory.

We finally ran Arturo to earth in Don Manuel's cabin. He opened the door quickly when we knocked, and Graciela started yelling a lot of uncomplimentary stuff in Spanish at him. It didn't seem to ruffle him. In fact, he looked less nervous than I'd ever seen him. He let Graciela continue her yelling bit until she ran out of breath, then quietly started explaining something about Don Manuel. Whatever it was, Graciela didn't seem to buy it. Aunt Kathleen watched the whole scene with a thoughtful expression. Finally she appeared to come to a decision, took Graciela by the shoulders, and firmly hauled her away in the direction of her own cabin. I tagged along with my head full of questions, and Arturo shut himself back up in Don Manuel's cabin.

As I had surmised, Aunt Kathleen was prescribing the Jameson Cure for Graciela's shattered nerves. We all three sat sipping the lovely stuff, and gradually Graciela's sobs subsided. I seized the opening.

"What was all that about, Aunt Kathleen?" I asked.

"As you could probably tell, Graciela was accusing yon skinny Spaniard of doing her godfather in. Arturo insisted that some business had come up that made it necessary for Don Manuel to fly to New York immediately. He's given Arturo his power of attorney to take care of his belongings aboard the ship."

"You mean he's trusting Arturo with his prize chickens?" I asked.

"I suppose so. Plus a fair amount of currently and such in the purser's safe, I'd imagine."

"It looks very fishy to me," I said. "When he was standing at the top of the gangplank, he sure looked like he was sweating out the minutes until Don Manuel arrived. How did he get the news of the Great Man's change of plans? By carrier pigeon?"

"That point wasn't entirely clear to me, but I assume your government is not so determined to keep Puerto Rico undeveloped as to forbid the use of the telephone there. What is plainly apparent to me is the fact Arturo was able to convince the captain to leave San Juan without his most important passenger. That power of attorney must be fairly convincing."

"There are such things as forgeries," I countered.

"Brian, lad, your prejudices, both con-Arturo and pro-Graciela are leading you astray. The captain's a canny man. He'd have verified the signature, you can be sure."

I wasn't convinced, but I couldn't think of any other objections at the moment, so I shut up and concentrated on the Jameson, while Aunt Kathleen explained her reasons for believing Arturo's story to Graciela. She didn't look any more convinced than I was, but she finally pulled herself together, used Aunt Kathleen's bathroom to restore her make-up, and went off to her own cabin. After thanking Aunt Kathleen for the Jameson, I followed her example.

Raoul was in my cabin, of course. No doubt he had stayed in his hidey-hole the whole time we were in port. There was also a new passenger, a big, broadshouldered guy wearing a few scars here and there on his heavy-jowled brown face. Raoul beamed as he introduced us in Spanish. I gathered this was a pal of his who was traveling from Puerto Rico to Veracruz wtih him.

I looked at the burly figure of our new cabinmate, and the light dawned. Now I knew why Raoul had smiled so happily the day before. Somehow he had got a message through from Santo Domingo to some of his political buddies, and they had provided this hefty hunk of flesh as a bodyguard. I looked him over very carefully. Even though the cabin was warm and stuffy, he was wearing a sports jacket, and there was what a triter writer than I would have described as a "suspicious bulge" near one armpit. Apparently the guy had all the requisite equipment to protect Raoul from any possible deck-lurkers who might still be around.

Then I began to wonder some more. We had lost one passenger in San Juan, and gained another. The one we had lost was a political enemy of Raoul's. The one we had gained was one of his gang. And this new buddy apparently specialized in physical violence. Had he used some of it on Don Manuel in some deserted San Juan alley? That might account for the glow of well-being Raoul was exuding. But how did Arturo come into the whole thing, then? I didn't think he and Raoul had ever laid eyes on each other.

I jittered my way through some pre-dinner drinks, feeling more and more uneasy about Don Manuel's disappearing act. Dinner brought something new to worry about. Elysia wasn't in the dining room. No matter how I loaded my stomach with nice fresh fish, tasty veal chops, feathery-light *flan*, the empty feeling that developed as I watched the place at the next table where I had expected to see her lovely head grew worse and worse. Where could she be? I knew she'd come back aboard. Aunt Kathleen and I had both seen her. I knew she wasn't prone to seasickness. So what the hell was going on? The Singdahlsen pessimism, fully revived, started champing at the bit.

After supper I intercepted Aunt Kathleen on her way to one of those gay terpsichorean sessions on the top deck and poured out my worries to her. She didn't help much. Even her indomitable optimism was having an off night. The best she could do was suggest that Elysia might be worn out by our day of beachcombing. About Don Manuel, she was strangely silent. I think she was feeling the same thing I was: something radically unpleasant had befallen the old man. I had no doubt about that now. The only question left in my mind were what, how and who. *Who*, I was sure, was the deck lurker. This time he'd been successful. Was he going to stop there? Or had he already gone further? Was that the reason Elysia . . . But even the Singdahlsen pessimism balked at that one. Elysia was all right. She had to be. Otherwise, what was the point of anything?

Aunt Kathleen, who had been occupying the deck chair beside me while I browsed through this gloomy reverie, gave a deep sigh, gathered her cape around her, and picked up her carpet bag. "Ah well, Brian," she said as she left me, "there's little we can do at the moment. Cheer up, lad. We may be making mountains out of molehills. After all, 'twill be all the same in a hundred years."

That didn't help much. Neither did the next day, another of those *Grew Bee* sunny days when all hearts seemed light but mine. Mine was occupied with Elysia, or rather the hole Elysia's absence made in my middle. I paced the decks all day hoping to see her slim figure curled in a deck chair. I craned my neck toward her table at breakfast, lunch and dinner. No trace. Finally, frantically, I sought out Aunt Kathleen and suggested we find out where her cabin was and make sure she was all right.

"A find neighborly idea, Brian. I'll go with you. As a matter of fact, I'd already wheedled her cabin number from the purser, with some such expedition in mind."

She led the way down the stairs, and I rapped on the door to Elysia's bottom-deck cabin. There was a little stir inside. Aunt Kathleen asked in her booming Spanish if everything was all right. Elysia replied in a tight, breathless, high-pitched whisper that did nothing very useful for the hole in my insides.

"She says everything is fine; she's just a little under the weather," said Aunt Kathleen. Her grim face told me she was no more reassured than I was. The door stayed obstinately shut. Evidently Elysia wasn't planning to invite us in. Aunt Kathleen shrugged her shoulders resignedly, and I followed her to her cabin, where we considered the situation over some therapeutic Jameson.

"The lassie's terrified," said Aunt Kathleen. "She's hiding out. What do you suppose has put such a fear on her?"

"It's got something to do with Don Manuel's disappearance," I said decisively. "It must have. Remember how gay and friendly she was in Puerto Rico? Then Don Manuel disappears, and Elysia immediately dives back down her mousehole. God, it's frustrating to be out in all this water, with no way of trying to find out what happened to the old geezer."

"I'll admit all this ocean does make one feel a bit hithery-thithery," said Aunt Kathleen. "Well, chin up, Brian. At least you know our Elysia is still with us. And I've a feeling in my bones that an hour or two on dry land, when we get to Caracas tomorrow, will give us some of the answers we're groping for."

As it turned out, we got one of the answers before we even set foot on dry land. While we were still tying up at the port of La Guaira, a pisspot-full of gold braid descended on the ship. I thought this was the standard immigration entourage, but then I noticed that some of the guys with the gold braid were speaking English—or rather, as Aunt Kathleen insisted on describing it, American. They turned out to be police officers from San Juan. The news they brought traveled around the ship like wildfire: they'd found Don Manuel.

106

While we'd been blithely coasting southward over the Carribean, the San Juan police had been fishing nasty corpses out of their waters. Or rather, one nasty corpse, but that one big enough and important enough to get the whole police force in a dither. Don Manuel had been found the preceding day, floating beside a dock, very very dead, with a switchblade knife still stuck in his back. Graciela had been right. This time whoever was out to get the big man had succeeded.

Now the police, of both Venezuela and Puerto Rico, wanted to question the passengers on the *Virgen del Toluca*. The brass set up shop in the first class lounge, and called passengers in for questioning one by one. Apparently they intended to go through the whole two hundred of us. Not alphabetically, though, because Arturo was first on the list.

Together with a lot of other curiosity seekers, I hung around the entrance to the lounge. I expected to see Arturo emerge white and shaken, maybe in handcuffs with a guard on each side. Not at all. After about fifteen minutes, he came out looking very calm. To my surprise, the next name on the list was Brian Singdahlsen. Wondering why they should pick on me, I quickly started checking out my alibi. It turned out that I was part of *Arturo's* alibi.

The police asked me if I'd seen Arturo in San Juan. I said sure, at the Mexican consulate. I added that Aunt Kathleen and Elysia had seen him too. After writing down the time I'd seen him and thanking me politely, they turned me loose, and then summoned Aunt Kathleen to the star chamber. Then came Elysia, pried loose from her hidey-hole by the official summons. She looked pale, drawn and tense, and glanced neither to the left or right as she went into the lounge and then scurried out of it back toward her cabin.

Even though I couldn't catch her eye, I felt a definite

lessening in the diameter of that hole in my middle. She might be scared out of her wits, but at least she was still alive, breathing, and free of any visible scars. Unlike that poor old chicken fancier, Don Manuel.

The police kept on talking to people—some assorted passengers whom I didn't know, a dining room waiter from first class, and finally Father Hernandez. They must have talked to everyone on board, but on most of them they spent so little time that it was clear this was merely a formality. Aunt Kathleen had been bird dogging the first bunch of questionees, and by dint of much exchange of gossip, had come up with a reconstruction of what the police had learned.

Apparently Arturo had come directly back to the ship after getting his visa, because he'd still been waiting at the consulate when we had left, at about eleven o'clock, and several passengers had seen him return to the ship at eleven-thirty. The waiter had seen him at lunch, and various other passengers remembered seeing him throughout the afternoon. Aunt Kathleen had it figured that the police had fixed the time of Don Manuel's death at sometime late in the afternoon, so Arturo's alibi was apparently all right. Father Hernandez had been the last passenger to see Don Manuel. The big man had offered the priest a ride in his taxi, and dropped him off downtown at about eleven. The padre had no idea of what he intended to do the rest of the day, though he remembered Don Manuel's mentioning the name of a business associate in San Juan. The priest said the police had seemed very interested in this clue.

Graciela appeared, accompanied by her husband who was trying unsuccessfully to suppress her current attack of hysterics. They went in for questioning together, and emerged very quickly, with Graciela still in tears. She headed for me and sobbed on my shoulder for awhile, with Victor looking on in a helpless sort of way. Finally she disentangled herself, and began a different sort of spiel, in which I was able to distinguish the world "*Adios*." I remembered then that she was getting off the ship here at La Guaira. This was goodbye, then. I felt a most unchivalrous flood of relief. I would miss her "berry nice" attentions, but the hysterics I could easily do without. Aunt Kathleen was hovering nearby, and came in with an explanation of what the stuff surrounding the "*Adios*" was all about.

"She's still convinced you're Sir Lancelot material," explained my interpreter. "She's convinced Arturo is the bad guy, and is telling you to see that justice is done." I told Aunt Kathleen to try to explain to the lady that Singdahlsen was the least likely of all available mortals to succeed in the nemesis bit, but so far as I could make out, my quasi-relative made no real attempt to do so. Graciela finally dried her tears, and went off to the tourist gangplank where Victor was superintending an assortment of feminine suitcases, hat-boxes, make-up cases and what not.

"I gave her a bit of the old blarney," said Aunt Kathleen, confirming my suspicion. "Told her you were the fastest brain on two continents and a close friend of Marshal Dillon. They have him on Venazuelen telly too, I gather. Put the poor Lassie's mind at rest. She was very fond of the old one, God rest his soul. Perhaps he was her godfather, after all."

"I'm sorry the old boy got dumped," I said, "but I'm more concerned with helping Elysia than avenging Don Manuel. Did you see how scared she looked? Do you think she's mixed up in Don Manuel's murder somehow? Is the guy who knifed him still aboard and maybe threatening her? And if he's threatening her, who else is he threatening? I'm beginning to get an uncomfortably vivid mental replay on that little judo session I ran into the night we left Tenerife."

"'This only human to think of your own neck first, Brian," said Aunt Ktahleen. "But there are other possible targets. Remember Raoul's suspicion that the attack on you was meant for him."

"Oh, Raoul's safe now. He's got his own personal bodyguard. A big tough character who came aboard in San Juan."

"Really? Now that's what you might call an interesting coincidence. I wonder what sort of story your new cabinmate told the police."

"Come to think of it, I didn't see him go into the lounge. I was sweating a little when Raoul went in, but apparently he didn't run into any trouble. But I'm sure his buddy wasn't questioned. I was keeping a special eye out for him."

"Don't tell me you're letting anyone replace your detested Arturo on the suspect list," said Aunt Kathleen. "You're suggesting your new cabinmate might have done the dirty deed?"

"Don't pull the incredulity act on me, my dear auntie," I said. "You yourself called his arrival a coincidence."

"You've caught me out, so," admitted Aunt Kathleen. "The thought did cross my mind—fleetingly, you might say—that a political comrade of our friend Raoul would have had reasons to rid the world of a certain bloated capitalist. Probably the police didn't question him because he wasn't aboard before the ship reached Puerto Rico. But that wouldn't necessarily mean he lacked acquaintance with Don Manuel. There'd be little way to proving any connection between them, though."

"I'm more concerned with what connection the murderer, whoever he is, might have with Elysia. Raoul's pal doesn't seem to fit it there. Elysia's been frightened during the whole trip. Whoever's frightening her must have been on board long before Puerto Rico.''

"You're making sense once more, Brian lad. Do you suppose this new reasonableness of yours will permit you to pry yourself away from the vicinity of Elysia long enough to enjoy a few hours ashore? She should be safe enough, locked in her cabin, and I have a great wish on me to walk about a bit on something more stationary than ship's planking.''

"Might as well,'' I said. "Who knows when I'll be in Caracas again? With all this talk about Venezuela nationalizing American companies, I have a feeling it may suddenly disappear from the standard tourist circuit.''

"I've always said it's the blessing of God Ireland has no oil wells,'' agreed Aunt Kathleen. "Come, lad, let's leave all this gloom behind us. The ship won't sail till almost midnight. On to Caracas!''

We took the bus that winds up through the green mountains to Venezuela's capital, and spent a surprisingly enjoyable day wandering around the city, eating some special sort of Sloppy Joe sandwiches at sidewalk stands and digging the contrasts between the old Spanish style buildings and the new skyscrapers. Like any city in the midst of a population explosion—name me one that isn't—Caracas was something of a mishmash. I felt it had lost most of its old personality, the food was gone. Also, the people were cheerful and friendly. All except one dude, some sort of policemen armed with a submarine gun, no less, who made a big scene when we started to walk into a pretty little park downtown. Aunt Kathleen finally got it sorted out.

"What this rather brusque peeler is trying to tell us, Brian, is that you are not dressed like a gentleman. In this part of the world, gentlemen wear suit jackets, even when it's boiling hot. In the middle of this wee park there's a building where Simon Bolivar, the famous Liberator, signed some constitution or other, so it's

111

sacred territory, and no peasant in shirtsleeves may enter its hallowed precincts."

"Even if I promise not to steal the ceremonial pen they have encased in gold there?"

"Don't be flippant, Brian. I must say this touch of old world formality appeals to me. The ancient traditions are slipping away fast enough in all the countries of the world."

"Peculiar sentiments for a rebel," I retorted.

"A true revolutionary seeks to preserve the good things in his country's history," she replied haughtily. "If you will excuse me, I shall go pay my respects to the memory of the Liberator."

She left me standing on the sidewalk outside the park, feeling a little pissed off. I started strolling around the block, keeping an eye out for the return of Aunt Kathleen. Suddenly someone slapped me on the back. I whirled. Was the guy with the submachine gun up to some more funny stuff? For one moment I felt an unprecedented spasm of sympathy with Dick Nixon, who had got himself stoned in this city awhile back, and not on grass, either. But it wasn't the cop. It was just our friend, Father Hernandez, being comradely.

I was glad to see a fellow traveler after walking through a city full of stranger. I managed to explain the cop's objection to coatless tourists, and the good father offered to lend me his sports jacket. Having worked myself into a mood as haughty as Aunt Kathleen's, I told him I wasn't particularly interested in walking in the footsteps of the Liberator, and he trotted off by himself to view the hallowed shrine.

He and Aunt Kathleen emerged from the park together, and at her suggestion he joined us in our travels around the city. Apparently he'd been there before. His running commentaries, translated by Aunt

Kathleen, whetted my flagging interest in the tropical metropolis.

Then I noticed something that killed all my interest in Father Hernandez' sightseeing spiel. Arturo was following us. He was doing it discreetly, keeping a healthy distance between us on the crowded sidewalks. But whenever we turned a corner, he turned it too, and once when we stopped in a cafe for a beer and another of those *Grew Bee* sandwiches, he must have lingered around someplace outside, because he picked up our trail again after we came out. I wanted to mention his presence to the padre and Aunt Kathleen, but I didn't, because I remembered her peculiar opposition to warning the priest when Arturo had trailed us in Santo Domingo. Anyway, I figured she already had Arturo spotted, and this time we were safely surrounded by thousands of Caracans, not isolated on a lonely tropical beach. All the same, I found my mind wandering away from the historical lecture Father Hernandez was handing out while I wondered what Arturo was up to now.

We had taken it for granted that the shadowing job in Santo Domingo had been done on Don Manuel's orders. But Don Manuel was dead now. So maybe Arturo had been up to some sinister trick of his own in Santo Domingo. Uneasily, I realized the cast of characters was still the same—Aunt Kathleen, Father Hernandez and me, with Arturo playing the heavy. Which of us was he after?

Aunt Kathleen finally admitted she'd had enough sightseeing for the day, and we caught the bus back to La Guaira. Arturo wasn't with us. I was glad he'd suspended his shadowing act temporarily. It had felt real spooky.

The padre and Aunt Kathleen had jettisoned the history lecture now and were chatting merrily away about Don Manuel's murder. I caught the name Victor Garcia and looked at Aunt Kathleen in surprise.

"Is he saying he suspects Graciela's husband?" I asked. "What chance would he have had to dump the old greezer, with Graciela and the whole wolf pack around?"

"The good father says that menagerie didn't stay together the whole day in San Juan. He himself saw Jorge and Victor by themselves in a gramophone record shop, no doubt adding to their collections the latest Yank assaults on the art of harmony. Graciela and her other admirers were nowhere in sight."

"Are we back to the old jealousy motive?" I asked.

"We are. You needn't look so scornful, Brian lad. Who should know better the lengths to which jealousy might lead than a priest, and he with the sins of the world pouring daily into his poor cranium like offal into a sewer?"

"But if Jorge was with Victor . . ."

"I asked the good father the same question. His opinion is that Jorge would be willing to aid and abet any act of violence against Don Manuel. He tells me your thespian friend is something of an anarchist."

So Father Hernandez had caught on to the reason for all those scowls Jorge had been handing him across the soup bowls. "He leans in that direction," I agreed. "I don't think he'd have the guts to try any murder stuff himself, but there's no doubt he'd clam up if he knew Victor dumped the old man. But look, if Victor did anything like that, Graciela couldn't help suspecting him. So why would she throw all those hysterics about Don Manuel's disappearance? It would have been more helpful to Victor of nobody had noticed his absence."

"Who says she'd want to protect Victor?" said Aunt Kathleen cynically. "A marriage certificate isn't a guarantee of undying loyalty, another fact for which the good father could supply much evidence, were his lips not sealed by his holy vows. But even supposing the hussy wanted to protect her husband—remember, she threw her fit just a few minutes too late to stop the ship from sailing. It could have been a ploy. Look at the effect it's had on you—it's making you argue in favor of Victor's innocence. Though of course, you're prejudiced where yon lassie's concerned.''

I didn't bother to bandy words about Graciela. Something else Aunt Kathleen had said had triggered the old Singdahlsen brain. "The really strange part is that the ship did sail without Don Manuel. And the reason the captain decided to sail was because of Arturo. You yourself convinced us of that. Now if Don Manuel was murdered, how could he send a message to Arturo saying he was staying in San Juan?''

"Arturo again! I swear, you've Arturo on the brain. Think, Brian lad. The old man could have been killed *after* he sent that message. If you're suspecting Arturo, remember all his movements have been accounted for.''

"Are you sure his alibi is airtight?" I asked. "There could have been a few minutes during the afternoon when he slipped away. The only person who could have been sure of seeing him leave the ship would have been the U.S. Coast Guard officer at the dock gate. It's interesting that Arturo managed things so he'd have several hundred miles of water between him and the Coast Guard men before the body was found.''

Father Hernandez had been listening intently during all this talk, and Aunt Kathleen now filled him in on what we'd been saying about Arturo. He nodded rather doubtfully, then said something to Aunt Kathleen.

"The good father says they'll probably show a photograph of Arturo to the guard who was on duty in San Juan.''

"Passport photos . . .'' I began cynically.

"Of course, a passport photo would make our own bonny Peter O'Toole look like Boris Karloff," said Aunt Kathleen. "But the police had their own photo equipment. They took a picture of the good father himself."

I was flabbergasted. "With all the suspicious characters floating around the ship," I said, "why would they want a snapshot of this harmless Chiclet dispenser?"

"Why indeed? The police mentality is unfathomable. I suppose it's that old chestnut you always read about in thrillers: 'Who was the last person to see the deceased alive?' " I noticed she didn't translate that last remark to the padre. Instead, she switched the conversation to some sociological chitchat about the palm-thatched shacks that perched on a mountain above us. I figured she wanted to cut off any conversation about the murder before we got to awkward questions from the priest like "Who was that strange man in dark glasses I'd never seen before?" Friendly soul that he was, I figured he'd made the acquaintance of everyone aboard, and when Raoul appeared for the police questioning, would have spotted him as somebody new.

The plight of the poor peasants was enough to keep those two occupied for the rest of the bus trip. We got back to the ship in time for dinner. All those sandwich things had destroyed my stomach's enthusiasm. Elysia wasn't at her table to provide food for my soul, so I skipped the last few courses and split early.

Arturo, now back in the tourist class dining room, had been piling into the food in his usual fast and furious way. I figured he'd been so busy tailing us that he'd come back aboard with an empty gut. I was more curious than ever about his continued concern with our whereabouts, but I hadn't yet had a chance to talk to Aunt Kathleen about him, as Father Hernandez had stuck with us through the pre-prandial sherry right up to the dinner gong.

I was gazing idly through the deepening twilight at the strung-out honky-tonk town of La Guaira, when Arturo came up from the dining room. He was headed aft in a determined way, and didn't spot me. I decided it was my turn to do a little tailing. Quiet as a ship's rat, I followed him. He headed for the lower rear deck. I followed, dodging between barrels of sherry and *acaparras*. He was heading for the chickens. He went up to their cages and did the Don Manuel bit, checking to see if all his feathered friends were feeling O.K. He even fed them bits of grain, though he was smart enough not to risk losing a finger. He poked the stuff as them with a piece of stray. They were drowsy now, getting ready for a good night's sleep so they could start their cock-a-doddle-do act bright and early.

I had just decided there was no point in continuing my surreptitious watch, since Arturo apparently was doing nothing more sinister than looking after his late employer's property, when another figure appeared beside the cages. It was getting dark now, but I could see that the new arrival was Father Hernandez, breviary in hand. He closed the little black book, marking his place with a ribbon as usual, and joined Arturo at the cages.

Arturo seemed friendly enough. An observer less astute than Singdahlsen would have thought he scarcely knew the padre. Certainly he gave no hint of any interest in him strong enough to explain his following the priest all over Caracas. They talked a little, and Father Hernandez cooed and talked baby talk to the chickens, but didn't offer any Chiclets, either to them or to Arturo.

I thought about joining them in their bird watching, but decided I was more interested in an old bird named Kathleen O'Connell just then. She should be finished with dinner by now. I went up the ladder to the main deck and found her comfortably ensconced behind a glass of *Quarenta y Tres* in a corner of the tourist class bar.

"Brian, *alanna,*" she yodeled as I entered. "I've been looking all over for you."

"You've given up on the daiquiri study project?" I asked, eyeing her drink.

"For the moment. The bartender tells me this delightful potion is unavailable in Mexico, so I mean to make the most of our last two nights aboard. There's plenty of rum in Veracruz if I decide to return to those lime-flavored bombshells."

That bit about the last two nights suddenly hit me. I'd begun to feel that the trip would go on forever. Now time was closing in.

"Have you seen Elysia?" I asked anxiously.

"Still holed up in her cabin. Talked to me through the door. Apparently she's still feeling poorly."

"Still frightened to death, you mean. At this rate, it looks like your matchmaking plans are shot to hell," I said morosely.

"Never give up hope, Brian lad. You'll remember she did talk of bathing with you on the Veracruz beaches."

"That was a whole two days ago, and she's avoided me like the plague ever since," I said. "Maybe it's me she's afraid of. Maybe she thinks I'm a vicious American mafioso who rubbed out Don Manuel."

"That's hardly likely, since she was with us all the time in San Juan."

"True," I said. "Except for . . ." I stopped there.

"Except for that twenty minutes after we left her downtown," said Aunt Kathleen. "Brian, you're becoming odiously melodramatic. Don't tell me you're thinking of that slip of a girl as a murderer. Why, she couldn't have so much as scratched the old tub of lard's little finger. It's ridiculous."

"It certainly is ridiculous," I said. "I guess this murder thing is getting to me. There are so many possible suspects—and the scene of the crime is far behind us. I try to tell myself it's none of my business, but I can't help wondering. Of course, Elysia couldn't have killed the old man, but what if she happened to see the murder? Maybe that's the reason she's been hiding out in her room ever since we left San Juan."

Aunt Kathleen wrinkled her formidable brow. "That's a thought has been bothering my old brain too, lad. It might be we'd be doing a great service to the lassie if we revealed the author of that crime. And wouldn't that put a bit of steam into your own courtship, now!"

"If the police haven't come up with an answer yet, I don't see how we can do better," I said mournfully.

"Ah, but the coppers don't know the people involved. We do. Let's put our heads together and go down the list again."

I didn't think it would do any good, but it might get her to loosen up with her ideas about what went on with Arturo and Father Hernandez. "All right," I said. "There's Victor, or Victor and Jorge; there's Arturo, there's Raoul, or rather Raoul's pal . . ."

I had expected her to object to such slander of her revolutionary pet, but she didn't bother. Instead she said. "You *will* keep harping on Arturo. Don't you realize he has the best alibi of the lot?"

"You know as well as I do he's up to something funny," I said. "Don't tell me you didn't see him shadowing us in Caracas."

"Naturally I saw him. I'm not blind yet. However, judging by his actions in Santo Domingo, it was probably the good father he was after, not two harmless bodies like ourselves.''

''If you're talking about harmless bodies, I'd certainly put Father Hernandez on the top of the list. So why should Arturo be skulking around after him?''

''You feel the good father goes about with a halo in his pocket?'' asked Aunt Kathleen, in a surprisingly acid tone.

''I didn't say he was a saint. Nobody is. But harmless, yes. I was watching him just now, talking Spanish baby talk to that bunch of feathered hoodlums on the lower deck.''

''He was with the chickens, was he?'' asked Aunt Kathleen, with unusual intensity. ''I thought the Chicken Fanciers Club met only in the mornings.''

''Apparently there's an evening session too,'' I told her. ''Arturo was already there when the good father came along.''

''Arturo too? And how did he treat the priesteen? Glare at him suspiciously or give him the evil eye?''

''No, that's what seemed so weird. They just talked casually, like any two shipboard acquaintances.''

''And your villainous Arturo, did he talk baby talk to the beasts as well?''

''He didn't talk to them. But he was feeding them, just like Don Manuel used to.''

''Feeding them! Was he now? That's most peculiar.''

''What's peculiar about it?'' I asked.

''If you don't know already, it's not myself will be telling you. I learned a bit about chickens when Sean Tracy and I were hiding out from the Tans in a chicken coop in Mullingar, County Westmeath.''

''Aunt Kathleen, you're being mysterious again. Why can't you trust your poor nephew with some of the wealth of secrets stored in the eccentric cranium of yours? First you hint that Father Hernandez isn't harmless; then you go all inscrutable about chickens."

"As to the moral condition of the good father," said Aunt Kathleen. "You yourself made a notable quip some time past about the habit not making the monk."

"You're hinting he's not all a storybook priest should be?" I asked incredulously. "Oh, come now. The kids love him, their parents beam at him, he's friends with everybody—and all those Chiclets!"

"We've a saying in Ireland: 'The darkest villain may give pennies to the poor.' " She pursed her lips thoughtfully. "Look at it this way, Brian. It seemed obvious to us that Arturo was following Father Hernandez in Santo Domingo on Don Manuel's instructions. That suggests Don Manuel suspected the priest of some sort of shady business. Then after his employer is murdered, Arturo follows Father Hernandez again. Doesn't that suggest he thinks the priest is the man who did the old man in? After all, your clerical friend admitted he was the last to see Don Manuel alive. And if you remember, he was one of the last passengers to return to the ship at San Juan."

"It makes a neat story," I said. "but the plot's much too weak to convince me that Father Hernandez is one of the bad guys."

"Scoff if you like, Brian. I've a few other reasons to doubt the harmlessness of the possibly unholy father, but your mind would appear too inflexible to accomodate them."

"Calling the Singdahlsen mind inflexible is like calling the rock of Gibraltar a sandcastle," I said. "I'm flexible as seaweed. I'll gladly match your dark thought for dark thought about all the sundry." A sudden memory stirred. "As a matter of fact, the first night I was aboard, I heard someone arguing with Elysia in a very nasty way. At the time I thought it was the padre, but I didn't know he was a priest. When I found that out, and saw all the love and peace stuff he was spreading around, I decided I must have been wrong about the guy's identity. But maybe it was Father Hernandez after all."

"You told me he was hostile toward you the next morning, didn't you?"

"Yes, down by the chickens. But I thought we'd decided that was because of his Saint Francis complex."

"Possibly. But you hadn't told me then about overhearing that quarrel. Did you catch what he and Elysia were quarreling about?"

"Not a word. My Spanish was absolutely nil at that point."

"The father might not have known that. He may have been talking about something very serious. Something dangerous to himself. That could explain the attack on you the following night."

"The attack on me? Now the padre's not only a magnate-murderer but a Singdahlsen-slugger?"

"Please demonstrate some of that vaunted flexibility of mind, my dear quasi-nephew," said Aunt Kathleen. "Do you recall a certain conversation with the priesteen following the first attack on Don Manuel?"

I flexed the old cerebral synapses. "I remember his saying something pessimistic about a priest being the potential third victim of the deck-lurker."

"That's right. But how would he know Don Manuel was the *second* victim? You'd told no one but the officials and myself about the attack on you, had you?"

"No one else," I said.

"And no one made any fuss about it, questioned anyone, or anything of that sort, did they?" she said intently.

"Not so far as I know," I said. "The officials treated me like a kid who's had a nightmare, and you were bound and determined to protect your precious Raoul."

"So how would the good father have heard of that attack—unless he himself were the attacker?"

"That's a neat use of the subjunctive," I complimented her, "but the idea's just too crazy. There's a lot of gossip on the *Virgen*. One of the crew might have said something to him."

"Possibly," admitted Aunt Kathleen. "But now let's take the subject of Elysia. You say you think it was the priest she was arguing with. Could it be that she's in deathly fear of him? Could that have been at the root of the startled fawn reaction?"

That was a blockbuster. It kept me quiet for a good three minutes while I went over in my mind the various occasions on which Elysia had demonstrated her fast getaway.

Finally I shook my head. "I don't think so," I said. "She's done her hundred yard dash lots of times when the padre was nowhere around. Besides, if it's him she's afraid of, why should she run away from me?"

"Perhaps he still suspects you of hearing something dangerous to him, something Elysia knows about too. He may have warned her to stay away from you."

"And you accuse *me* of melodrama!"

"Don't dismiss the idea too lightly, Brian. Let's explore the problem of Elysia from another direction. When *hasn't* she dashed away from you? When has she been really amiable?"

I could answer that with no trouble at all. "That's easy. There were two times she was absolutely charming to me. First in Tenerife, before Arturo messed things up, and then in Puerto Rico."

"You see? Both of those times we weren't aboard the ship. That meant there was a good chance she could talk to you without the likelihood of Father Hernandez coming around the deck at any minute."

"They why did she dash off in Tenerife?" I objected.

"Who was it came and joined our table shortly after she left?"

"The padre and his cub pack, of course," I said. "But how was Elysia to know he was headed our way?"

Aunt Kathleen gave me a withering look. "Sometimes I think you've less wits than God gave a toadstool, Brian," she said. "Of course it was Arturo who warned her."

"Possibly," I said grudgingly. "But why? What's the connection between Elysia and Arturo? That time in Tenerife was the only time I've ever seen them even notice each other. The rest of the time they've acted like strangers."

"True enough," said Aunt Kathleen. "I've no theories as yet on what their relationship might be, but I'm sure there is one. If we could puzzle that out, we might have the key to Don Manuel's death."

"Maybe you'd better go a bit slower on the *Quarenta y Tres,* Aunt Kathleen. It seems to make your mental processes unintelligible to us ordinary mortals."

"You're implying I have no logical reason to make the statement I just made," said Aunt Kathleen. "I'll admit that. It's just that I have a feeling in my bones that Elysia and Arturo are connected in some very important way. And since Arturo was so obviously close to Don Manuel, he probably knows more then he's telling about his patron's death."

"Like where he bought the switchblade," I said.

"You're still insisting he's the murderer. I'm sure he's not. I've a feeling . . ."

"In your bones, I know. Spare me the Gaelic mysticism, Auntie. Let's let this decrepit piece of bone Singdahlsen calls a brain take a rest. I'll join you in that innocuous-tasting anesthetic."

We settled down to some serious sipping, but amnesia refused to set in. I couldn't stop thinking about Elysia.

Was she really clinging to her cabin because she was terrified of Don Manuel's murderer? I couldn't swallow Aunt Kathleen's sudden certainty that Father Hernandez was one of the bad guys. But I had sensed an undercurrent of fear in Elysia from the very beginning of the trip. She was certainly frightened of something or someone, and she had taken to her cabin with strange abruptness just at the time Don Manuel had disappeared. It seemed very likely she believed she was in great danger. Was she really marked as the next victim of Don Manuel's killer? The thought made my blood run cold. That graceful, gentle girl was no match for the kind of people who know where to get switchblades and how to use them. She needed protection. God knows I'd been serious when I'd assured Graciela that Singdahlsen's muscular prowess could be piled on the head of a pin. But at least I could try. Even if the blue-eyed beauty disappeared from my life forever once the *Virgen* reached its final port, at least I could try to protect her until then. I thought of curling up in front of her cabin door like a watch dog, but decided that *would* be melodramatic. She was probably safe enough so long as she hid out there. The thing to do was to let her know I was avilable for bodyguard duty when she finally had to leave her retreat.

I think Aunt Kathleen sensed the turmoil in my mind, because she sipped her liqueur thoughtfully and silently, with none of her usual ploys to goad me into conversation. Despite four of the potent glasses, I was still sober as an undertaker when the ship's engines began to throb around eleven o'clock and the *Virgen* moved away from the dock. We both went out to the rail to watch the lights of La Guaira fade slowly into the black velvet night. Then we went our separate ways.

When I got to my cabin, I found Raoul nad his hefty chum still awake and looking very unhappy. They were discussing something in low tones. I gathered there was some sort of problem connected with our landing in Veracruz. Raoul tried to explain it to me, throwing in some more of that *enemigos politicos* stuff, but I couldn't make out the nuances of this particular political crisis. Evidently they'd got some kind of bad news while we were anchored in La Guaira. It must have been something pretty heavy to make the stand-in for Rocky Graziano look so unhappy.

I finally got them to go to bed by saying several times, "*Manana—Senora Oconaya*," which was the way Raoul always referred to Aunt Kathleen. The promise that we'd enlist that wily old rebel's help in the morning seemed to soothe them, at least to the point of turning off the lights. The *Quaranta y Tres* sneaked up from its hiding place and did the rest. I slept like a well-sedated log all night, and didn't even dream about Elysia.

CHAPTER 6

Next morning I was up at cock crow. Literally. When I heard the familiar chorus of cock-a-doddle-dos, I bolted out of bed, hoping I wasn't late for the morning session of the Chicken Fancier's Club. After all, it was our last day at sea, and besides, it was a pretty sure bet I'd find Aunt Kathleen there and have a chance to summon her to the aid of her beleaguered fellow-rebels.

She was there, all right, bright-eyed and bushy-tailed. She was pretending to concentrate on her favorite rooster, a full-throated specimen who held the ship's record for sustained noisemaking. Knowing her as I did, I was sure her attention was really elsewhere—on the spirited conversation that was going on between Father Hernandez and Arturo.

"A very interesting development, Brian," she murmured to me out of the side of her mouth. "The good father is making his move for the welfare of captive chickendom. He's just made Arturo a handsome offer to buy the whole lot."

"Sounds like a windfall for Arturo," I said. "Without Don Manuel to train them, no one would have much use for those musclebound fowls."

"You'd think so, wouldn't you," said Aunt Kathleen. "But it seems he doesn't intend to sell. Listen to him. His temper is up, for some reason."

I listened to Arturo. I could only make out a few words here and there, but their essence was clear. Arturo was telling Father Hernandez it'd be a cold year in hell before any of Don Manuel's chickens would be allowed to set foot in *his* rectory garden.

"Why that note of personal animosity, I wonder," I said to Aunt Kathleen. "Don't tell me you've been unloading your poisonous thoughts about the good father to Arturo."

"Still the skeptic, are you, Brian?"

"Where the young priest is concerned, I am. Aren't you a little ashamed of those thoughts now? Here you've been painting the padre as a deep-dyed villain, and it turns out what's really occupying this thoughts is the welfare of these restless roosters."

"When the fox lingers by the chicken house, it's not because he's in love with the hen, Brian."

I saw it was useless to argue. Once the proverb stage set in she was beyond reason. Besides, Father Hernandez wasn't in any danger, whatever dark thoughts an eccentric Irish lady might be directing at him. Raoul was. Aunt Kathleen might be able to dream up some helpful little scheme for him.

"Auntie," I said, "would you mind coming down to my cabin for a few minutes? There's something important I want to discuss with you."

She caught on immediately. "Why of course, Brian lad. It's a strange time of day for a man to be luring me into his den but at my age I can't be choosy, can I?" She started threading her way between the barrels toward the stairs. I thought Father Hernandez was staring at us a little suspiciously, but then decided my mind had been poisoned by all Aunt Kathleen's mysterious claptrap.

When we were out of earshot, Aunt Kathleen dropped back beside me and murmured, "It's our friend

Raoul who wants to talk, is it not?'' I nodded. She smiled in a satisfied sort of way, like a horse returning to familiar pastures. We didn't speak again until we were inside my cabin, where Raoul and his pal—I'd gathered his name was Jose—were polishing off the last of their morning coffee.

Raoul's face brightened when he saw Aunt Kathleen, and he introduced her to Jose with what sounded like a lot of flowery compliments. His spiel was good enough to make Jose relax and stop thinking about that gun in his shoulder holster. Raoul then launched into a lengthy description of the problem that had them both uptight, or so I judged from the frequent *enemigos* and *peligrosos* with which he peppered his monologue. Aunt Kathleen popped in a few questions here and there, and eventually nodded her head in an understanding way.

'' 'Tis a familiar problem, Brian lad. They've learned there's an informer in their ranks. It's very like the time Seamas Gallagher caught young Denis Clarke slipping information to the constabulary about Michael Collins' hideout. It seems one of their organization has informed the reactionary party of the false name under which our man is travelling.''

"They plan to make trouble for him with the Mexican immigration people?'' I asked.

"Lord, no, Brian, nothing that innocuous. Our friend would have little difficulty with the Mexicans. Their government has a firm policy of protecting political exiles, particularly those hounded out of their countries by dictators. No, our friends here believe their enemies intend to set up an ambush. Since Mr. Lucho's features are not all that well known, particularly without the facial shrubbery, they need someone to point him out to the assassins. The Judas kiss, as it were. Raoul's guess is that someone may have bribed a Mexican official to give some signal when he comes through the immigration line. That's why it was important for his opponents to learn the name of his false passport."

It sounded pretty hairy. I would have accused Aunt Kathleen of lapsing into melodrama again, but I figured she knew more about the politics of the gun than I did. And I'd read the papers often enough to realize that assassination was beginning to overtake football as the number one world sport.

"Any idea what we can do about it?" I asked.

"Nary a one at the moment. I'm scraping the bottom of my antiquated cerebrum, but nothing comes up except muck."

"You must have had some experience in slipping a man through official barriers," I said.

"Naturally. But we had all sorts of useful stage props that don't exist here. I mind the time young Keather Hernandez. What the hell was he doing listening at keyholes? Could be he *was* one of bad guys as Aunt Kathleen insisted? But why *our* keyhole?

While I was mulling this stuff around in my head, Father Hernandez had launched into a combined apology and explanation. He didn't look half so embarrassed as I would if I'd been in his shoes. Aunt Kathleen and the two men listened to him with all the cordiality of a bed-tempered cobra for a few sentences, but as he went on they began to look surprised and interested. Finally the men broke into delighted grins, and Jose pulled his hand out of his jacket and slapped the good padre on the bad with comradely enthusiasm. Aunt Kathleen wasn't smiling as much as the other two, but she looked interested and receptive.

"What the hell's going on here?" I asked. "A guy stands around listening through keyholes to dangerous political secrets, and all of a sudden he becomes our number one buddy. What gives?"

"A most interesting turn of events, Brian. The good father was explaining that he had come looking for me because Dona Herlinda the rich biddy in first class, wanted to secure my address for the purposes of correspondence. He was just about to knock when he inadvertently heard our conversation about the peril of our friend here. Naturally, he hesitated to interrupt. But now he tells us his Christian sympathies have been aroused, and he is volunteering to help the man we call Raoul to elude his assassins."

"For Christ's sake!" I exclaimed.

"Exactly. The way the priesteen put it was 'Although my religion forbids me to kill in order to help the poor, I am willing to risk dying for them.' A rather noble sentiment, I must admit. Worthy of our own Robert Emmett."

It did sound like a good line. With a little polishing, maybe I could fit it into something like the stuff Graham Greene used to write. Or how about a revival of the Bing Crosby-type padre story? That was more in the Chiclet-scatterer's style. "Very noble indeed," I said. "What do you think now about all that stuff you were handing me last night? Still think the priest's a secret deck lurker?"

She had the grace to look abashed. "Perhaps I was too hasty, Brian. At any rate, this turn of events makes me willing to, shall we say, suspend judgment."

I thought that was a kind of lukewarm attitude toward somebody who had just volunteered to risk laying down his life for a stranger. But then, nobody likes to admit his mistakes. "Just how does he plan to carry out this sacrificial act?" I asked. "In any other country, he could lend our friend a cassock, and smuggle him in as neatly as that nun you mentioned. But Mexico has cancelled out cassocks."

"There's no need for costumes, Brian," said Aunt

Kathleen. "The passport's the thing. Our friend and the padre are similar enough in appearance to make a switch of passports possible. The priest will enter Mexicon under the dangerous name the assassins are waiting for. Our friend will enter as an innocuous member of the Mexican clergy. If there *are* assassins waiting, it is Father Hernandez they'll follow. He plans to mingle with the crowd long enough for Raoul to make his exit safely, then head straight to the police. By the time he's explained his true identity, Raoul will be in safe place where his friends can protect him."

"A neat scheme," I said admiringly. The padre, Raoul and Jose were chatting animatedly together. I stuck out my hand to the priest. "*Mucho bueno*," I said fervently. "*Usted hombre magnifico*!" My praise made him turn on his boyish smile and wave his hands in a depreciating way. I felt exhilarated and happy. There were some pretty good people left in the world, I thought, and a lot more important things going on than Princess Anne's wedding and the opening of a new boutique in Chelsea. It seemed as though the bonds of the piddling little life I'd been leading for so long all snapped free at once, and I was living in a new, much realer world.

Then I remembered Elysia, and my vow to protect her. It was obvious now that it wasn't Father Hernandez she was afraid of, but the fear was definitely there. It was up to Singdahlsen to do something about it.

"Aunt Kathleen," I said. "Shall we leave these three to discuss ways and means of foiling the villains, and find ourselves a quiet spot of deck?"

"If you'll accompany me in a detour to my cabin to collect my carpetbag," my counselor replied.

"Sherry at this hour?" I exclaimed, the Singdahlsen suavity going down the drain once again.

"In moments of crisis, Brian, sherry at any hour. We haven't quite reached the Jameson stage, but I think I

132

know the problem that's occupying your mind, and it definitely rates a glass or two of Tio Pepe if we're to deal with it effectively."

I acquiesced meekly, and we soon settled down in some isolated deck chairs to do the glass and bottle routine.

"It's Elysia you're thinking of, is it not, Brian?" said Aunt Kathleen after a few preliminary sips.

"That's right," I said. "I'm getting more and more certain that the reason she's holing up in her cabin is that she's terrified of something or someone."

"I've good news for you, so. I've managed to breach the lassie's defenses. We had a long talk in her cabin last night."

"You've talked to her! Why in hell didn't you tell me that right away?"

"Now, my lad, you must ride that impatience of your with a tighter rein. This is the first chance we've had to talk by ourselves. Besides, I was meaning to withhold my news until nearer the moment of crisis. But I see you're hellbent to hear it this very moment."

"Crisis? What crisis?"

"Slow down, lad, and let an old lady tell the story in her own meandering fashion. As I was saying, I managed to see Elysia in her cabin. Followed the steward when he came to collect her tray and barged right in like the traditional pig in Kelley's parlor. I told her straight out I knew she had a great fear on her, and furthermore informed her that you and I wanted to protect her from whatever was troubling her. I hope I didn't take liberties in using your name?"

"Of course not. You know I want to help her. But go on, what did she tell you?"

"She finally admitted she was indeed afraid for her life. She wouldn't tell me who she's afraid of. Says he's vowed to kill her if she breathes a word to anyone. She's sure he's the man who murdered Don Manuel, and wouldn't boggle at another murder. She believes she's safe so long as she stays in her cabin, but she's frightened that tomorrow, when she has to leave the ship, the rascal will attempt to do her some harm."

"Do *you* think she's safe in her cabin?" I asked anxiously. "If you managed to get in with the steward, someone else . . ."

"The steward is a fine strong figure of a man, and Elysia's given him strict orders to keep out of each and every male visitor. He was just about to give *me* a fierce clout, but seeing I was a harmless old biddy, he restrained his hand. No, she's safe enough until the landing. That's when the crisis will come. You have your work cut out for you, lad."

"He can hardly attack her in broad daylight with people milling around. Or can he?"

"Probably not. What she fears most is he'll follow her after she leaves the customs building, then bide his time and attack her in some lonely place in Veracruz. I've assured her that you and I will see her safe to her hotel and stay with her until we can arrange to have the villain detained by the police."

"The hotel bit sounds fine. There's nothing I'd like better than watching Elysia on a round-the-clock basis."

"From a discreet distance, I trust. We'll alternate watches, four hours on and four hours off. 'Tis the best way to remain alert, as I learned to my sorrow when we were waiting for some smuggled guns in Leenane harbor, County Galway. I was so sure I could watch the whole night through, but my eyelids betrayed me, and if Dan Gannon hadn't had the good luck to wake in the middle of the night and see the signal lights . . ."

"Please, Aunt Kathleen, let's write your memoirs some other day. What I want to know is how we're going to get the police to collar this guy. Has Elysia got proof he killed Don Manuel?''

''Nothing the courts would call proof, though she say she's absolutely sure . . .''

''The police aren't going to act on the word of one poor frightened Spanish girl.''

''Well, now Brian, I have my own ideas as to whom the villain is, and I think I've a surefire way to summon up the interest of the police in him. But 'twill take some time. A few days, perhaps.''

''You're being mysterious again, my dear aunt. For once, won't you come clean and tell me the whole plot?''

''I've told you before, Brian, that your open face would give you away.''

''Then it's someone I'm likely to see? Someone I'll be in close contact with?''

''Draw whatever wild conclusions you like, my lad. I'll speak no further. My lips are sealed.''

''Then it must be someone at my table. Elysia's never acted scared of Jorge. Father Hernandez is out—he proved it with that magnificent offer to help Raoul. That leaves the dude I've suspected all the time, Arturo. Right?''

''When Kathleen O'Connell seals her lips, they remain sealed.''

''Very well, my distinguished and widely experienced old clam,'' I said. ''Singdahlsen can do some lip-sealing too. I promise Arturo will get no hint from me that we're onto him. But I still don't see how you're going to get the police after him. After all, that power of attorney he says Don Manuel gave him was good enough to fool the captain.''

''Never mind the ways and means. I promise you I have a trick or two up my sleeve. I'll try to join Elysia as soon as she gets through customs. We first-class bobs will naturally be speeded through much more quickly than you tourist class serfs. You make a threesome with us as soon as you can, and we'll head off to the Hotel Bolivar, making sure that no one follows us.''

"Hotel Bolivar," I said. "I don't like the omens. Bolivar was the guy who got me into that nasty beef with the Caracas cop.''

"It's the only hotel Elysia knows. Her father used to stay there on business trips. She's sure it's well away from the center of town. Less people coming and going, fewer dark alleys. If we're separated for any reason at the customs house, we'll all rendezvous there.''

"Right on, madame commandant," I said.

"So much for safeguarding Elysia," said Aunt Kathleen, downing the last of her Tio Pepe and pouring us another one. "Now we must plan your part in safeguarding Raoul.''

"Me safeguard Raoul?" I said. "But I thought that was all set. Changing passports with Father Hernandez should get him past any funny business from a crooked immigration official. Besides, he's got Jose to take care of the strong-arm stuff.''

"Yes, and once he's through immigration he has his own large group of political associates who'll see him safe. The tricky period is the immigration line. There must be no chance of the immigration people detecting the switch in passports.

"That should be safe enough," I said. "He and Father Hernandez are the same height and build, and passport photos all look pretty much alike.''

"The problem lies elsewhere, Brian. You know how popular the priesteen is on board ship. He's well known to everyone. Suppose one of the other passengers standing behind him in line sees that the passport he's using bears the name of Raoul Alvarez instead of Julio Hernandez? Mightn't he raise a fuss?''

"I don't know. He'd probably assume the priest had his own reasons . . ."

"Assumptions could bury us, Brian. We must make sure. It will be simple for you to take the place in line behind Father Hernandez. Then you'll be the only one in a position to accidently observe the change in passports. Jose, of course, will be behind Raoul, so that's no problem."

"But I should be with Elysia," I protested.

"Time enough for Elysia later. Now, please, enough of this carping. It's necessary at this point to place yourself completely in my hands and let me make the decisions. That's the primary rule of a successful revolutionary, following orders."

"The last time I placed myself completely in someone's hands, he promised me a peaceful and undisturbed voyage," I said. "It hasn't exactly worked out that way."

"You're sorry for that, are you? Sorry you had the horrible fate of meeting the lovely Elysia! Sorry to have the chance to help a brave patriot!" Scorn blazed in her eyes. She looked as if she was about to demand the return of her Tio Pepe.

"Of course I'm not sorry," I said vehemently. "Life feels a lot more real these days than it has for years. All right, even though you won't trust me enough to drop even a crumb of information about all your mysterious plans, I'll trust you. I'll follow orders. It may be an utterly insane thing to do, but that kind of insanity has apparently preserved *you* to a ripe . . . maturity."

"Don't pussyfoot, Brian. It's bad for your prose style. When you mean *old age*, say old age. Age is the kindest enemy I've encountered thus far in my life. And speaking of age, I think the morning is well enough advanced that we might partake of a heartening portion of the fifteen-year-old Jameson. You know, 'tis one half of our Irish description of bountiful hospitality: 'The youngest of food and the oldest of drink.' "

The day passed in a pleasant haze of Jameson, San Miguel and *Quarenta y Tres*. Elysia wasn't at her table for lunch or dinner. I had stopped worrying about that. Her absence meant she was safe in her cabin.

Arturo wasn't there either, so I didn't have to practice my poker face. Probably he was holing up for a bit of anticipatory knife sharpening. I hoped all the cabin stewards who were providing room service for Raoul, Jose, Elysia and Arturo would get suitable tips. *Somebody* should be getting some benefit out of all this weird mishmash.

Needless to say, I got no writing done that day.

CHAPTER 7

We sailed into Veracruz harbor just after sunrise the next morning. From a distance, the city looked almost as good as Peter's propaganda. Once inside the barrier reef, the water was clear, calm and turquoise-colored. To our left a tiny island exhibited the promised palm trees, ringing a small lighthouse. Ahead, I could see stretches of beach along the shore where the city curved around to meet us. There was nothing that a Californian would call smog, only a light haze softening the contours of the many-colored buildings.

The waiters had laid on the coffee and rolls at dawn. Lots of early birds were clustering around the top of the gangplanks with their hand baggage as we eased slowly into the pier. Raoul and Jose were well in the forefront, just as planned. I found Father Hernandez, and we edged into line a safe thirty passengers away from the man who was using the priest's passport. Aunt Kathleen had explained my protective function to him, and the padre smiled and chatted amiably to me while dispensing the ultimate ration of Chiclets to all his young admirers.

I looked around for Elysia. She was standing beside the stairway to the dining room, looking scared to death. I tried to catch her attention, but she was staring apprehensively down at the deck. That pale, woebegone look aroused all my protective instincts. I resolved that as soon as I'd got Father Hernandez safely through the immigration formalities, I'd wait for her to come through and attach myself to her immediately. *This* time, if Aunt Kathleen had explained our motives clearly enough, there could be no startled fawn routine to inflict its damage on the Singdahlsen ego.

The immigration bit took place on shore this time, instead of on board ship. The Mexican officials looked uniformly bored, but did their paper work efficiently. I breathed a sigh of relief as I saw Raoul move away unchallenged form an official passport stamper, followed by Jose. He then headed for the other side of the big stone hall to go through customs. He had only one suitcase, so there should be no hold-up there. Father Hernandez and I moved steadily along the immigration line.

An official reached for the priest's papers. I felt tense all over, but maintained the old poker face. Father Hernandez looked like any happy tourist. The official hardly glanced at the documents, merely checked his entrance visa against the name on the passport, did a bunch of stamping, and handed the papers back. The priest moved on.

Then it was my turn. The official looked at the passport picture more carefully this time. Clearly he was wondering what a gringo was doing among this mob of Spanish-speakers. He read all the fine print, tilting the passport sideways to decipher the signature of the Secretary of State, looked at all the immigration stamps—Greek, Turkish, Dominican, English, Venezuelan, U.S.—and then handed back my Mexican visa and the passport reluctantly, as if he was wondering if he ought to detain me for questioning as an international spy. This was fine with me, as it gave Father Hernandez plenty of time to make his escape. I hadn't noticed any funny business when the officer had read

Raoul's name on the passport the priest carried, but there was no use taking chances.

To my surprise, the padre had made no visible attempt to flee the scene. He wasn't even heading for the customs section, where passengers' baggage from the ship's hold was now being stacked under the initial letters of their last names. Instead, he was waiting just outside the immigration barrier.

I thought about joining him to find out why the change of plans. Then I decided it would be better to get my own customs business over with so I'd be free for action. Since I only had one big old suitcase and my typewriter, that shouldn't slow me down much. I could see Elysia now. She was near the end of the immigration line. By the time she came through, I should be free to join her as planned.

As I stood in the customs line, I had a chance to observe that the people who went through fastest were those who unobtrusively tucked some sort of currency into the inspector's hand. Peter hadn't told me the protocol on this, but I decided to take a chance on a fifty peso bill. The tan-uniformed dude who got it frowned a little and said something in Spanish. I did the *no comprendo* act, hoping I wasn't going to be charged with attempting to bribe an officer, but he just shrugged his shoulders, rummaged around in my suitcase lackadaisically, scrawled some chalk marks on my unopened typewriter case, and that was that. (I learned later from Aunt Kathleen that the going rate was a hundred pesos, but the dude probably didn't want to tackle the job of explaining this delicate point to an illiterate gringo.)

Now legally free to walk out under the promised palm trees, I looked around for Elysia. She had just cleared the immigration line. I went over to join her. Father Hernandez reached her just before I did, smiling and talking. She was looking very frightened, but stood where she was and answered him. Was there a gleam of welcome in the glance she gave me as I came up to them? I couldn't be sure. It was Father Hernandez I was worried about now. Why was he still here? Why hadn't he split immediately as we had planned? If Raoul's enemies were lying in wait for the guy carrying his passport, every minute of delay increased his chances oif playing host to a bullet or a knife.

It suddenly hit me that our melodramatic scheme was no kid's prank. It had all seemed so simple yesterday. One good guy, Father Hernandez, getting another good guy, Raoul, out of a purely temporary little mess. But now something was going wrong with our lighthearted game. Father Hernandez wasn't playing his part right. Didn't he know that any minute he could become very dead?

And dumb old Singdahlsen couldn't even speak enough Spanish to remind him his life was up for grabs. Frustrated, I looked around for Aunt Kathleen. She was over in the customs section, among the baggage from the hold. Elysia started over toward the customs line, and Father Hernandez followed her. "Damn it, Padre," I felt like shouting at him, "why don't you get the hell out of here!"

I wanted to get hold of our commandant, Aunt Kathleen, but on the other hand, I didn't want to get back behind the customs barrier and risk getting hung up again, so I stood kind of helplessly, looking from Elysia to Father Hernandez to Aunt Kathleen. Then I noticed something funny. Aunt Kathleen wasn't in the "O" section where the O'Connell baggage would presumably be stashed. She was over the "R" section. Arturo was there too. Since when did "Urbino" begin with an R? Very peculiar goings on. I'd already decided Arturo was our bad guy, and I didn't like the idea of his hanging around that close to any of my friends.

Then I saw the explanation for Arturo's presence there. The chickens! The cages of Don Manuel's fighting cocks had been just brought ashore and were stacked under "R" for Rodriguez., No doubt Arturo was playing his role of trusted secretary to his deceased patron and pretending to look after his property. But then what the hell was Aunt Kathleen doing there, when she should be joining me and Elysia? And why was she arguing so intensely with the tan-uniformed guy with the mustache who looked as if he was getting really fed uop with this crazy foreign lady's line of talk?

Suddenly all hell broke loose. Aunt Kathleen reached into her carpetbag, pulled out a small shining object, cut a rope around one of the cages, grabbed one feathered hunk of fury by his neck and swung him round and round in a circle. He flopped and struggled, then went limp. I'd seen that trick on the farm in Petaluma, when my uncle wanted a chicken for our own table. Swing it around and break its neck. Less blood than using an ax, and usually quicker. But it takes a pretty strong wrist. Apparently my surprising travelling companion had strong wrists.

I moved closer to see what was going to happen next. Aunt Kathleen wasn't through. Now she was using the pocketknife with which she'd opened the cage to slit the dead rooster's throat. What the hell? Why offer the customs men an impromptu chicken barbecue? And it wasn't even her own chicken.

Now she was pulling a handful of something out of the chicken's throat and showing it to the customs man. The angry look on his face suddenly turned to interest, then to a kind of happy excitement. Completely forgetting my concern about Elysia, Father Hernandez, or the customs barrier, I rushed over to see what was happening. The official was examining some small pebbles he held in his hand, wiping them off on some straw from the cage, and rattling away in rapid Spanish to a crowd of his colleagues who had gathered around him.

"What the hell is all this?" I growled in a low voice to Aunt Kathleen, who was standing there as peacefully and complacently as if she'd just finished her first Tio Pepe of the day.

"Uncut diamonds, my dear Brian. I daresay you've never seen them before. I've only had one other chance to observe them, the time in '21 when we made payment to some Belgian gun merchants in that medium."

"Uncut diamonds in a chicken's throat?" I screeched, sounding remarkably like one of my feathered neighbors in the cages.

"In his gizzard, to be exact. A very clever way of smuggling contraband jewels. Instead of gravel, provide your rooster with a box full of rough diamonds. He's bound to pick up enough to make the trip worthwhile."

"But don't they shit them . . . er, I mean, don't they pass the stones out through their intestines?"

"Oh, they do shit out the occasional stone, Brian, after they're worn down from their function of grinding food for the chickens. But these are *very* hard stones indeed. Hardly likely to be worn down sufficiently in a three weeks' journey. And if they are expelled, it's a simple matter to get them back into the gizzard again."

Staggered by the scope of this business, I said, "Then all these babies are choking in diamonds? You're talking Aga Khan language now."

"The *aduanales* will determine that. But I think your surmise is correct. We're dealing with a sizeable fortune in diamonds here."

"And Arturo knew it! That's why Don Manuel was killed. So Arturo could take over the birds with his phony document!"

I looked around for Arturo. He had disappeared.

Then, suddenly remembering that he was the guy Elysia was terrified of, I looked for her. She was standing just outside the customs barrier, looking very pale, but not quite so frightened as before. Father Hernandez was no longer with her. I couldn't see him anywhere in the big stone hall.

I breathed a sigh of relief. That uproar about the chickens had been a godsend for him. It had made a great cover for his getaway. Unfortunately, it had given Arturo a good chance to split, too.

I looked back at Aunt Kathleen. "We've got to get Arturo, Aunt Kathleen. Can't you tell these dudes to put out an all points bulletin or whatever they call it?"

But Aunt Kathleen was surrounded by a sea of tan uniforms and brown faces, all smiling brilliantly and obviously sayiong some very complimentary things about "*la señora irlandes.*" Then some other Mexicans in civilian clothes joined the group. It looked like they were detectives. I figured Aunt Kathleen could handle anything that was happening there, and headed for Elysia.

She smiled at me warmly, and now appeared completely relaxed. Of course, I thought, it was Arturo all along. Now that he's gone, she's not afraid. I still thought it was a good idea to get her out of there, and said in a masterful way, "*Vamos al Hotel Bolivar.*" She nodded enthusiastically and started toward the exit. I tried to signal to Aunt Kathleen, but she was still immersed in that flood of official adulation. Oh well, she knew where we'd be.

Elysia strode purposefully down the broad steps outside the customs building, carrying a large handbag and a small suitcase. She waved to a taxi, we climbed in, she gave directions. I watched Veracruz whizzing by, catching sight of a flower-laden plaza surrounded by sidewalk cafes, narrow streets full of stores, another big plaza, a broad boulevard with two rows of palm marching down the center divider. The cab stopped and we climbed out. Elysia paid the driver before I could collect my financial wits. I looked around. All I could see were big residential-type houses. There was no sign of a hotel. I looked inquiringly at Elysia. She smiled and led me to a stone bench in the park that divided the boulevard. There was a fountain there with live flamingos in it.

"It's a beautiful day, to be sure," I said to Elysia, who was calmly looking around her in all direction. "But is this the time for a sightseeing trip?"

She understood my English well enough. "*Momentito*," she said. "I be sure no other person go with us." I caught on. She was using one of the standard detective-story methods of avoiding a tail.

After a few minutes of observation, she was apparently satisfied that no one had followed us. She hailed another cab, and this time I could clearly catch the words "Hotel Bolivar." We were finally back on madame commandant's schedule. I relaxed and started figuring out how to prove to Elysia that it was necessary to her safety that we should share not only the same hotel but the same hotel room.

The taxi whizzed along a few residential streets, racing from light to light in a pleasantly daredevil fashion. All of a sudden the bay was in front of us, turquoise deepening to sapphire, with frills of white foam breaking the sparkling surface here and there. We sped along a seafront drive, then swung right for a block and jerked to a stop.

The Hotel Bolivar offered a long blank yellow wall to the sidewalk where we climbed out. This time I managed to beat Elysia to the draw and paid the fare. But once inside the festively tiled lobby, my nerve failed me, and I let her handle the room rentals. Naturally, I wound up

146

in solitary splendor next door to the double room Elysia engaged for herself and Aunt Kathleen.

I looked hopefully for a connecting door, and found one leading to a balcony. I stepped out on it. The view was great. A block of rooftops in front of me, then the sparkling blue of the Gulf. It was enough to sidetrack me from my lecherous quest for a good three minutes, at the end of which Elysia forestalled me by emerging from her room onto the same balcony. She had changed to a gleaming white sleeveless dress which set off her shipboard tan in a mouthwatering way.

She smiled. I smiled. I couldn't think of any way of saying what I needed to say to her. Here we were, alone at last in an exotic foreign port, no longer surrounded by a shipload full of interested bystanders. Now was the moment for the offhand offer of a cigarette, the narrowed eyes, the sexy voice, the casual arm encircling her shoulders. Bogart would have known how to do it. I knew too, but the Singdahlsen motor reflexes seemed to be temporarily paralyzed. I guess some of this came through in my smile, though, because Elysia suddenly grew shy and turned away, leaning over the balcony as if looking for something in the street below us.

Then I remembered that she had a good reason besides shyness to peer at the street. The chicken business had supplied Arturo with a first-class motive for killing Don Manuel. Elysia had said Don Manuel's murderer was after her. And Arturo was still at large!

Fine bodyguard I was turning out to be. I should have been sweeping the street systematically with my tiny pair of high-powered Zeiss binoculars. Not possessing this essential item at the moment, I had to retrieve my knight-errant status by glaring balefully down at the pavement two stories below us with my own patented stop-'em-in-their-tracks glare. Meanwhile, I mentally cased the joint and started mapping out our plan for defense, still keeping a watchful eye on the street below.

We were on the third floor; there were no rooms above us. There was only a single row of rooms on our floor, all opening onto the balcony we were standing on. From the hotel, the only approach was the stairway from the lobby and the long narrow corridor with room doors opening from it alone one side. From the corridor outside Elysia's door, I should be able to see the top of the stairway. I made a mental note to check out the possibility of a second stairway. I didn't think there was one. Now, what about this balcony we were standing on, overlooking the street . . .

My watchdog reverie was suddenly interrupted by a squeal of brakes as a taxi raced by the intersection on my left and ground to a halt out of sight in front of the Bolivar's entrance. I was pretty sure Elysia's pursuer wouldn't announce his arrival so blatantly, but it provided a good excuse to move closer to her, and then to follow her back into her room. She was evidently unalarmed by the new arrival, because she had the door to the corridor open and stood beside it with an expectant smile. In a minute or two, a bulky tweed-enveloped figure hove in view at the top of the staircase, and Aunt Kathleen, puffing a little from the climb, let out a delightful war shoop: "Up the Republic! *Sinn fein amhain*!"

"Very neat work, Brian my lad," she continued, lowering the decibels a few hundred as she came nearer to us. "I knew we could count on you to keep the lassie safe. Now we're all cozy and snug here together, three against the world." She strode past us into the room, gave an appreciative look around, and ensconced herself in an arm chair while the porter stowed away her three big leather suitcases in the ample closet. When he had gone, she looked at us with a familiar twinkle and reached for the carpetbag at her feet. In companionable silence, we watched as she brought out a silver flask, unscrewed a stack of silver cups from the top of it, poured a shot of Jameson for each of us, and leaned back to savor the warming potion.

"That was quite a show you put on at the customs house," I observed, once my vocal chords were suitably loosened.

"A notable victory, indeed, though I say it myself."

"You're very handy with that wrist and penknife routine," I added.

"Learned it as a child on my grandfather's farm in Dunbeg, County Clare," said Aunt Kathleen. "Used it to good effect one night in a barnyard in Mullingar, County Westmeath when a noisy goose almost brought the Tans in on us. Now *that* took a bit of strength, you can believe me. Geese are much more ferocious beasts than chickens, you know."

"How in hell did you know the diamonds were there?" I asked.

The familiar "not telling all I know" look appeared on Aunt Kathleen's craggy face. "Well, 'tis this way," she murmured. "My mother had the gift of the second sight, do you see . . ."

"I'm not buying that," I said, "I know you tell well. You've got some perfectly ordinary explanations you don't choose to reveal at this time."

She had the grace to look abashed. "You're right, Brian," she said. "There was nothing supernatural about it. For one thing, I was curious about all the attention those birds commanded. The chicken growers I have known never mooned over their flocks like your little shipboard club."

"It was something to do. There wasn't much excitement on the ship," I began defensively, then broke off, remembering the two knife attacks and a murder weren't exactly monotony.

"To be more specific, I noticed Don Manuel doing something peculiar. You remember how he'd hand feed the chickens? That seemed to be a strange thing for him to do, since I'd observed their appetites needed no spur. When I watched him carefully, I soon tumbled to the fact it wasn't corn he was handing them, but pebbles. I thought then the pebbles must be very precious indeed for them to be fed to the birds one by one. Then Don Manuel was murdered, and Arturo started 'feeding' them. The whole thing came to me in a flash."

"Still, it took quite a bit of nerve to put on that demonstration for the customs officials."

"What was I to do? The blathering eejits wouldn't listen to me. I had to show them. Though I will admit, after they'd seen the first handful of diamonds, they were quick to the slaughter. Feathers flying every which way, as they did in two more just to make sure."

"More diamonds?" I said.

"Lahings of them," said my aunt. "The old tub of lard must have had a direct pipeline to South Africa."

"You think Arturo knew about them?"

"Of course. Why else would he take it upon himself to 'feed' them?"

I was suddenly alarmed. "Aunt Kathleen, are you sure he didn't follow you here?"

"Follow me? Arturo? No, Brian, *no one* followed me, Arturo or anyone else."

"Anyone else? What do you mean, anyone else! You're the one who turned up Arturo's motive with your chicken-sticking act. Obviously, Arturo learned about the stones Don Manuel was smuggling, disposed of his fatcat boss, and produced a convincing forgery to give him possession of all those diamond-happy birds."

"That's your readind of the situation, Brian?" She was going all inscrutable again.

"Of course it's my reading. It's yours too, whether

you admit it or not. Arturo's the one certified bad guy we have around, and if he's after Elysia, we have our work cut out for us keeping her safe. We'd better start figuring out our defense strategy.''

"No problem there, Brian. Not so long as we have my good companion here to keep us safe.'' She reached into the depths of her carpetbag and came up with a dented but serviceable old Luger. "A little souvenir of my younger days,'' she said fondly. "And this little trinket might help also,'' she added, diving again.

This time she came up with a small cowbell. "What do you suggest we do with that?'' I asked caustically. "Play a tune on our criminal's cranium?''

"You spoke of strategy, Brian,'' said Aunt Kathleen reprovingly. "Have you forgotten the element of surprise? Picture our unknown assailant, creeping quietly and, as he thinks, unobserved on his nefarious mission. Suddenly a terrible cacophony of cowbells shatters the midnight calm and his nerves as well. It'll be as effective as a Gatling gun, and much less messy.''

"Not a bad idea,'' I told her grudgingly. "Now, where do we park ourselves with this arsenal?''

"We've little to worry about here in this hotel, Brian. The door from this room opening onto the corridor is all we need to guard.''

"There's a bit more to it than that, Madame Commandant. You see that other door? The one right across from you? And the window beside it?''

"Don't be insulting, Brian. You imply I've lost some of my faculties. Of course I see that door and window. They open onto the balcony over the street. I saw that as I drove up, and took the precaution of enquiring from the desk clerk about that balcony, pretending to be the usual weak-livered English tourist. He was quick to assure me there's no access to it from the street.''

"How about from the roof?''

"Covered with broken glass, he tells me. Quite sufficient to deter any ambitious cat burglar."

"Arturo is playing for higher stakes than some local hoodlum," I said.

"You're right, Brian lad. We mustn't be lulled into false security. Why don't you go inspect the premises from the balcony and see for yourself how the land lies."

I jumped at the opportunity to display my knight-errant repertoire. Leaving the two women together, I did a thorough job of inspecting the full length of our balcony. The balcony below ours was pretty far down, but I thought someone with climbing tackle might make it up from there. He'd have to do it at night, though, because during the daytime hours there was a steady sprinkling of pedestrians and cars below us. Any funny business with ropes would be sure to attract an admiring audience.

I looked at the rooftop, and realized that, too, would be a tricky proposition from Arturo's point of view. There was a wide overhang above our balcony; the roof stuck out a good three feet beyond our balcony rail all the way along. Even without the management's trusty broken glass on the roof, it would be almost impossible to swing in far enough to be sure of landing on the balcony. Of course, with ropes it might be possible. I didn't know just what opportunities the buildings on either side of the Bolivar offered for someone to climb onto our roof. Still, if I sat on guard in the corridor with both the inside and balcony doors to the woman's room open, I should be able to catch any sounds of monkey business from the balcony. Judging from the way the sun was boiling through right into my bones now, the nights would be balmy enough that a bit of extra cross-ventilation wouldn't cause them any discomfort.

I went in and gave my report to Aunt Kathleen, who

nodded in satisfaction. Elysia was looking preoccupied and somber. "There's one bright spot to all this," I said, hoping to cheer her up. "Our little scheme to get our friend Raoul through the barrier seems to have worked. Your sideshow with the chickens sure helped both Raoul and Father Hernandez to slip away without any fuss. Strange to think we'll probably never see either of them again."

My cheer-up effort wasn't working. Elysia looked even more somber. Then I remembered she had never met Raoul and his pal Jose, and probably didn't have the slightest idea what I was talking about. And yet, when I mentioned Father Hernandez, the worried look had darkened into downright gloom.

Aunt Kathleen was picking up on Elysia's dark mood too, and doing her cryptic best to join my cheer-up campaign. "We've an old saying at home, 'Mountains don't meet; people do.' I'd not be so sure we won't see more of those shipboard companions of ours."

Her observation didn't seem to reasure Elysia any more than my feeble effort. I wondered why the hell Father Hernandez' disappearance should bother Elysia. Had she liked the priest all that much? Suddenly I remembered the argument I'd overheard the first night on board. I figured our newfound alliance against the world would cover a little nosy effort on my part to make a positive identification of the guy who'd been so nasty to her. "I hate to bumrap the hero of the hour," I said, "but there was one thing about the good padre that bothered me. Elysia, that first night out from Cadiz, I thought I heard him arguing with you."

I figured she didn't need a translation, because her smile suddenly came back to life, and she almost laughed. The memory of that Singdahlsen nosedive to the deck must have been a pretty comic one.

"*Si, es verdad,*" she said. "Padre Hernandez berry

angry that night. But is really not important. We have small fighting about religion; the Church, *entiende*? I do not believe as he does. It is night, we have been drinking wine. So we talk berry strong, *muy furioso*. Next day, all is different. Padre Hernandez say he is sorry. All is—*como se dice—oividado*."

"All forgotten," said Aunt Kathleen. "Water under the bridge. Surely you've had your share of experience with these nighttime arguments that fade with the sunrise, Brian? They're one of the national sports in my own dear homeland."

So it was as simple as that. I remembered how I had stupidly let my imagination conjure up some sinister relationship between the priest and the girl, had been type casting him as Mr. Hyde. Well, at least I had been more rational about him than Aunt Kathleen had, with all her dark suspicions. I'd quickly abandoned my unfounded grudges against the guy who'd turned out to be an authentic hero in our unheroic times. I still thought his risk-taking on Raoul's behalf was the neatest scheme I had come across in years.

My recall of the image of Singdahlsen spread-eagled on the deck had achieved my objective, cheering Elysia up. She was still smiling reminiscently, and I was sure only politeness kept her from giggling audibly at the memory. "Now all the bad times are past," she said. "We are here in this fantastic city of Veracruz. Let us have fun! We must eat, we must drink, we must see everything!"

"That's the spirit," said Aunt Kathleen. "After all those days pining away in your cabin, you deserve a change. Brian lad, we're going out on the town!"

I was dubious. I knew we weren't out of the woods yet. Both women seemed to be ignoring the very real threat of Arturo, who was probably as adept in the dark alleys of Veracruz as he had been on the deck of the

Virgen. Still, the trick with the chickens had put the police on his trail. Arturo would hardly make any move in bright sunlight or well-peopled places. And I certainly didn't want to say anything that would bring that somber look back to Elysia's lovely eyes.

To clinch the deal, the word "eat" had set the old enzymes flowing, and I suddenly realized I was ravenous. Visions of luscious Gulf shrimp danced in my head. I threw myself enthusiastically into the cab-securing bit, and in no time at all the three of us were sitting in one of those fabled sidewalk cafes on the main plaza, looking past palm trees and flowers at the baroque facade of the Palacio Municipal, listening to a marimba band while a white-jacketed waiter bestowed Margaritas on us and disappeared to tell the cook about the boatload of shrimp we were planning to feast on.

Sidewalk cafés are great for lingering. We lingered over the Margaritas, we lingered over the shrimp, we lingered over the coffee and brandy. Then we wandered; through the flowered plaza, down to the Malecon, a wide promenade jutting into the bay, from which we could inspect ships from Norway, Sweden and Japan riding at anchor, plus our recent home, the *Virgen de Toluca*. It seemed strange to see her decks empty of people. I wondered how soon she would start on her return voyage to Cadiz. Personally, I had no intention of heading back to the Old World for a while yet. The sunshine, the palm trees, the Gulf of Mexico, the sidewalk cafés, the marimba bands, and Elysia—there were plenty of attractions to keep me here in Veracruz for months and months. I sent a mental blessing to Peter, drizzle-bound in grey London, for kicking me out of purgatory into paradise.

Lingering, it seemed, was what one did in Veracruz. We lingered on the Malecon, watching the ships and the water, then back to the plaza to linger some more over more Margaritas. ("So good for you in a hot climate, all this salt," said Aunt Kathleen.) As we downed a tasty seafood soup, the sky darkened and the lights came on; the Palacio Municipal, outlined in light bulbs, glowed like an electric cobweb. Still we lingered, savoring a last glass of *Presidente* brancy, now a rival to Jameson in Aunt Kathleen's affections.

Then we took a swift cab through the quiet, flower-scented streets back to the Bolivar. While the women settled themselves into a night of welcome sleep, I sat in their doorway with the Luger on my knee and the cowbell beside me, a watchful eye on the corridor and an ear cocked toward the outside balcony, helped immeasurably by Aunt Kathleen's thoughtful provision of a thermosful of hot tea which she had magically obtained from one of the waiters at the café.

"I had him brew it the way the lads on watch liked it in the old days," she said, "strong enough to trot a mouse on. 'Twill keep you eyelids aloft til the sunrise comes to your rescue."

The tea was surprisingly effective. I only dozed off a couple of times during the uneventful night. Aunt Kathleen came wide awake with the first rays of the sun, and volunteered to take over the watch. I wandered out in search of breakfast and found a sidewalk café around the corner. The black coffee tasted good after all that tea, and the bacon and eggs seemed almost as ambrosial as yesterday's shrimp.

A newspaper vender came by. I bought a paper and browsed through the columns of Spanish, calling a few familiar names here and there—*Estados Unidos,* Kissinger, *petroleo, Arabes* . . . Then a sudden chill went through me as another name swam into view, a name known to me privately, but to few other people. *Raoul Alvarez Paredo.*

Haltingly I inched my way through the paragraph.

Even with my minimal Spanish, I could make out that the name now belonged to a corpse. A corpse with a passport bearing Raoul's name. But of course, it wasn't really Raoul who was dead. Raoul was still safe. Raoul was safe *because* this man was dead. The man who had volunteered to switch passports with Raoul to save him from his enemies was dead. The enemies had been more tenacious than we had thought. Father Hernandez had made his sacrifice.

CHAPTER 8

I finished my breakfast and walked back to the hotel in a mental fog. It had suddenly hit me that if it hadn't been for me, Father Hernandez would still be alive. After all, I was the one who had dragged Aunt Kathleen into Raoul's problems. If I hadn't brought Aunt Kathleen along to my cabin that morning to help Raoul, Father Hernandez wouldn't have eavesdropped and made that noble offer. That's what happens, I told myself bitterly, when you step outside your nice safe observer slot and get into the action. Not only does your writing get goofed up, but you leave a trail of disaster behind you.

Just as I was renewing my resolve to crawl back into my shell and leave all the action to the other guys, I saw a familiar figure emerge from the hotel entrance half a block away. Arturo! He looked both ways, and then started walking away from me towards the beach. He hadn't spotted me. I realized the tropical sun was behind me, and had probably partially blinded Arturo when he looked my way.

My decision to return to hermit crab status took a sudden reversal. My heart started hammering. Had he already reached Elysia, evaded or overpowered Aunt Kathleen and made good his threat to kill the girl? Did his casual exit from the hotel lobby mean he'd engineered some sort of trick attack that left him free to walk out, leaving a trail of corpses behind him, with no fear of apprehension? I started to run toward his retreating back, with some crazy idea of wrestling him to the ground and calling a cop, then suddenly checked myself. I had to see Elysia first. She might be wounded, in need of quick medical help. Catching Arturo wouldn't do her any good if she was bleeding to death upstairs right at this moment.

I took the stairs at a gallop, grabbed open the unlocked door of the women's room, and plunged through it. Then I came to a surprised halt. Aunt Kathleen and Elysia were sitting there quietly, Aunt Kathleen reading a book, Elysia combing her long shining black hair in front of the mirror. They both stared at me in surprise as I made my abrupt entrance. I breathed a sigh of relief. So Arturo hadn't been in the room after all! Probably just casing the joint. That was bad enough, but it meant we had a chance to take some extra precautions.

"Brian, lad, what's the trouble?" asked Aunt Kathleen. "You come bursting in like a demented cyclone and then fall into a trance, with never a cheery greeting for either of us."

"Sorry," I said lamely. "I just saw Arturo leaving the building, and I was afraid he'd hurt you."

Aunt Kathleen lifted an eyebrow. "Arturo was here? What a pity he didn't manage to talk to us," she said blandly. I was about to tell her what I thought of her blithe unconcern for Elysia's safety, when I was distracted by an enchanting smile from Elysia. She seemed to be as cool and unperturbed as Aunt Kathleen. Was everybody nuts?

Still, with that curtain of silky black hair as a backdrop, the smile was enough to rock me on my heels for a second or two. "You are berry good, Brian," she said. "I am berry glad you take care of me." My whirling brain registered that this was the first time she'd called me by name. A pleasant tinge of contentment crept into my outraged apprehension.

"We're safe as churches here, as you can plainly see," said Aunt Kathleen. "Whatever your man Arturo was up to, it's meant no harm to us. Won't you have a chair, and perhaps a drop of the craytur to soothe your nerves, which are clearly all at sixes and sevens."

I gratefully accepted a seat and the silver cup of Jameson she handed me. "All the same, we'd better be extra cautious," I said. "Maybe we should find out from the room clerk if Arturo asked where our rooms were."

"Never you mind all that hanky panky, Brian. I've already given the desk clerk full instructions on that score, backed with a tidy gift of currency."

"Arturo could have bribed him with a tidier one," I said mournfully.

"I think not. I took the liberty of displaying the personal calling card which Captain Ramirez of the customs service was kind enough to present me with yesterday. Apparently he wields a great deal of power in this city. No enemy of ours will get any information from the management, you can be sure."

I relaxed even more. I should have known Aunt Kathleen had thought of everything. Then I glanced at the newspaper which I still clutched in one hand, and remembered the sad news.

"I was already upset before I saw Arturo," I said. "It looks as though Father Hernandez didn't make as clear a getaway as we had thought."

Aunt Kathleen gave a little exclamation and reached for the paper. She spotted the key paragraph immediately and read it carefully, then handed the paper to Elysia.

"Found knifed in an alley," she said. "The poor man. A nasty way to go." Her comment sounded strangely casual. *She* didn't seem to be feeling any pangs of guilt for involving Father Hernandez in the scheme that cost him his life. I glanced at Elysia. She was staring fixedly into the mirror, her face white and immobile. The news had clearly been a shock to her. I went over and offered her the last half of my whiskey. She shook her head as if to clear it, then drained the silver cup to its dregs, and took a deep breath.

"A sad event," she said. I nodded silently. Our eyes met in the mirror, and Elysia's lips curved into a shaky smile. My guilt complex disappeared. Suddenly I became aware of the bright sunshine shining in the window, the fresh smell of the sea and the dancing palm trees along the beach front. It was too bad Father Hernandez had to be dead, but we were alive—the two of us—and it was a beautiful day in a beautiful city.

The voice of our chaperone broke the spell. "Your color looks better, Brian lad. Not so much resemblence to the belly of a dead mackerel. I'll leave you here to guard Elysia, so, while I put in an appearance at police headquarters. I promised I'd come down and give them a statement this morning. Now, with this new development, I must see about correcting their identification of the corpse."

Again, there was the casual offhand tone when she referred to our dead hero. It grated on my sensibilities. I reminded myself of all the corpses she must have seen before she turned twenty. She had good reason to grow a thick skin. I promised to stay with Elysia till she returned. Surprisingly, I wasn't at all sleepy. I realized I was operating only on love and adrenalin, but I'd never felt better.

We put Aunt Kathleen into a cab and then wandered down to the seafront, where Elysia had breakfast in a palm-thatched restaurant built out over the water. An hour went by, two hours, we watched the people on the neighboring beach, and talked in fragmentary Spanish and English. The water was shallow, only waist high to most of the bathers. I thought of going back to the hotel for bathing suits, but was to contended to move.

Then Aunt Kathleen bustled in, having caught sight of us from her homebound cab. "A perfect spot for our mid-morning sherry," she cried. "I feel it's well earned, after all the business I transacted this morning."

"You set the police straight about Father Hernandez?" I asked.

"I didn't need to. They'd already been told about the case of mistaken identity. When they found yesterday's date stamped by the immigration official in the dead man's passport, they called in the ship's purser, and he identified the body as the good father's. No one could account for the fact that he was carrying another passenger's papers, though, and needless to say, I didn't enlighten them on that score. I did add a few contributions of my own, which they're going to follow up. Then I made my statement about the chickens, and that was that. A good morning's work." She had the delicate stemmed glasses out now, and was pouring the sherry. The waiter didn't seem to mind. I figured he was inured by now to any sort of strange behavior on the part of gringo tourists.

"How about Arturo?" I asked. "Are the police on his trail?"

"Never fear, Brian. They've already got a warrant out for him, because of his connection with the chickens, and Don Manuel's murder too. I put a few more fleas in their ears that will help straighten things out." I thought she was being purposely vague, but I'd learned there was no use pushing her. She had to have her little mystery.

As we sipped our sherry, I resolved that if I ever saw Arturo again, I would bring this whole cops-and-robbers game to a rapid close. Singdahlsen's showdown. I visualized myself holding a trembling Arturo at bay with Aunt Kathleen's ancient gun. "This is it, Arturo. You're in bad trouble . . . ." I wondered if he spoke English. It would be a shame to have my high moment of drama spoiled by the lack of a translator.

Aunt Kathleen's voice broke briskly into my reverie. "Now all that sordid business with the police is over with, we've the whole day ahead of us," she said. "Those delicious prawns yesterday merely tickled the surface of my appetite. I could do with another such meal, couldn't you? Captain Ramirez gave me the name of an excellent seafood restaurant down in the market district."

"Sounds like a great idea," I said. "Let's grab a cab."

"A bus, this time, I think," she protested. "Just as quick, I understand, and a fraction of the price. If I'm to manage those thousands of miles to New York, we must pull in our financial horns a little." She led the way authoritatively to a bus stop. A rattling little green-and-red bus chugged to a halt in front of us. "All the busses running along here wind up in the market district sooner or later," said Aunt Kathleen. "A peso and a half will cover the three of us." I dredged up a handful of change, and the smiling driver picked out two coins and nodded to me. We sat on hard wooden seats and watched the city rush by. The bus filled up with passengers. Then all of a sudden, it started to empty, as women with bright-colored nylon mesh shopping bags pushed toward the front door.

"Here we go, lad," hissed Aunt Kathleen, joining the pushing throng. We climbed out into a busy downtown street. While Elysia and I were still looking around,

Aunt Kathleen had spotted our destination. "There it is, my children. *El Puerto de Alvarado*. Just down the street." She led the way along the crowded pavement, past several market stalls stacked with flowers of every color under the sun, then up a narrow stairway to the second floor. A glimpse through a central corridor behind the flowers showed me the restaurant was in the municipal market building. We emerged from the noisy jostile of the street into the leisurely calm of the restaurant, and snagged a table by a window. From here we could watch the milling throng below in comfort.

A nearly church bell chimed noon. The Veracruz lunch hour doesn't start til two, so we were early. The restaurant was ready for strays like us, though, and our platters of broiled shrimp appeared in record time. Finally sated, we leaned back and sipped coffee, still watching the seething mob below.

Suddenly a chill ran down my spine. A dark head had just turned away from a shop window across the street. I breathed in sharply. A standard Latin type, I told myself. Merely a chance resemblance. Nothing to get excited about. But as the slender figure in the next grey suit turned full-faced toward me, looking up and down before crossing the street, I got a clear view of his face. Chance resemblance, my ass! It was Arturo! I scrambled to my feet, pushing my chair back with a clatter.

"Arturo's down there," I said. "I'll catch him. You line up a cop, Aunt Kathleen."

She opened her mouth to say something I didn't hear. I was already half way down the stairs. I hit the pavement half a block from the spot on the sidewalk where Arturo had paused after crossing the street, and headed straight for him.

Suddenly he saw me coming and whirled, heading away from me, weaving through the jostling crowd at a rapid pace. I picked up speed. So did he. It was rough going with all those people. A woman carrying a live turkey by its legs scowled at me as I bumped into her. I apologized to her and the bird, and kept going. I managed to keep Arturo's figure in sight. Then he pushed into the middle of a clump of people at a bus stop. I saw his head and shoulders rise out of the mass as he squeezed through the door of a blue-and-white bus. I caught up to the edge of the crowd shoving toward the bus and came to a standstill. There was no way of pushing through. The bus was jammed full already. Its doors closed just behind Arturo's grey-suited form.

The crowd started flowing to my left and I flowed with them toward another bus that had screeched to a stop in back of the first one. It was blue-and-white too. The sign above the driver's head read "Zaragosa." Was it heading in the same direction as Arturo? I had no idea. But the people who had been pushing toward Arturo's bus were now thrusting their way into this one. I fished out a peso and hoped for the best.

The bus was filling up rapidly. If I didn't make this one, I was sunk. Arturo would disappear again, and the whole damn cat-and-mouse game we were playing with Elysia's life would go on indefinitely. I shoved harder through the crowd, using my elbows in some rude maneuvers not calculated to encourage good hemispheric relations. I made it into the bus, grabbed a pole, and hung on for dear life as the driver swung his machine around a traffic circle and then headed out a side street.

Were we following Arturo? My spirits rose when I saw a blue-and-white bus a block ahead of us. Arturo's bus? I wasn't sure, but I thought so. There was only one passenger jammed between me and the door. I kept my eye on the bus ahead, ready to jump when Arturo did.

We jolted to a stop, and started again. Once, twice, five or six times. The residential streets sped by. A few women climbed down from the bus ahead, but no Arturo. I clung grimly to my pole. What if I was mistaken and Arturo was now speeding off in a completely different direction?

Then I saw the sea front. That was confusing. I was sure the bus we'd taken to the market was red-and-green. Did the blue-and-white once go to the same beach? It sure looked like the boulevard we'd watched during Elysia's breakfast, palm trees and all. Maybe Arturo was heading toward the Bolivar. Maybe the room clerk, primed by Aunt Kathleen, had turned him away earlier that morning and he was now trying an indirect approach. I cursed myself for not checking out the buildings on both sides of the Bolivar. If he reached a neighboring roof and managed to get to our balcony, he could find some corner to hide in and explore the place at his leisure. But he'd guess I'd alerted the women before I started chasing him. He couldn't be so crazy as to head toward the Bolivar now we had seen him!

I realized with a jolt that he might not even be on the bus ahead of me. We were passing the public beach now, with the palm-thatched restaurant just beyond it. There were more beaches ahead, secluded ones with no bright canvas chairs or umbrellas, and only a few scattered bathers.

Suddenly I tensed, and started banging on the door. The bus ahead had stopped, and a lean grey-suited figure had jumped out. My bus driver threw me a glance of good-natured exasperation and ground to a halt in the middle of a block. I lept out, almost falling to the sidewalk, but managed to maintain my balance. Arturo had dashed to the seafront side of the boulevard and was climbing over the low concrete wall that edged the beach. I ran out in front of a slow-moving black Renault and made it safely to the beach side, vaulted over the concrete wall, and landed six feet below in soft sand.

Arturo was racing along the beach toward a stone breakwater that stretched a long narrow neck into the bay. I followed him. There was more beach on the other side of the breakwater. Arturo headed toward the water. Now he was splashing into it, still fully clothed, first knee high, then waist high. Six or seven small boats lay at anchor in the protected cove formed by the breakwater. A larger boat, a launch with a cabin, was tied to a post on the breakwater. Arturo was heading toward one of the little boats. He climbed aboard a bright red one and reached out for the anchor line. Something in his hand sparkled in the sun. The anchor line snapped as he cut it.

I was knee deep in the water now, heading for the boat nearest to me, a green one. I pulled myself aboard and at the same moment heard the roar of an outboard engine. I looked up. Arturo and the red boat were moving rapidly away from me toward the open sea, leaving a white froth of water fanning out behind. I looked for the motor on my boat. There wasn't any! Just a couple of narrow oars. Even if the Singdahlsen muscular prowess had been Olympic class, I would have been no match for the outboard.

Then I heard a familiar voice: "Up the Republic! *O'Connell abu*! I turned toward the shore. Running toward me across the sand was a familiar bulky figure, green cape billowing, carpetbag clutched in one hand. Just as she reached the shore, I heard another voice shouting in Spanish behind me. It came from the larger boat with the cabin. A little man was jumping around furiously on deck, shaking his fist at Arturo's departing back, shouting a stream of words that were obviously curses.

Aunt Kathleen changed direction and ran out on the breakwater toward the angry little man. She shouted something to him that I didn't hear. Suddenly he stopped cursing and started helping her aboard. She waved a beckoning arm to me. I jumped out of the green boat and waded toward the little man's launch. I heard an engine starting. Then my hand grasped a rope ladder. I climbed up onto the launch and sat squishily on the deck for a few minutes, catching my breath.

I realized we were moving swiftly out into the bay. Arturo's red boat was a small blob out near the horizon. The distance rapidly narrowed between us, and the red boat grew bigger and bigger. His small outboard motor was totally outclassed by the little man's engines.

Aunt Kathleen was beside me. "Brace up, Brian lad. You started a hare we must run to earth. It'll be only a few minutes more."

"How did you get the little man to join the chase?" I asked, when my breathing finally slowed down to normal.

"*Join* the chase? Damnation, lad, our new friend Pepe is *leading* the chase. Hell has no fury like a capitalist robbed of his property. The boat Arturo made off in belongs to Pepe, and he needed little urging to set out in chase of it. I suppose Captain Ramirez's card may have helped a trifle, but your man Pepe was already—how did that scruffy Yank guitarist put it—oh, yes, 'hot to trot'."

We were getting very close to the red boat now. I could see Arturo clearly. He was crouched over the back of the boat, trying to coax the little motor to put on more speed. His eyes were wide with fear as he stared back at us.

Suddenly he gave the rudder a sharp turn. The red boat jerked around and headed toward the shore.

"Look what the bastard's doing," I yelled. "He's

heading for land. He's trying to beat us to the beach and take off on foot again!''

I had to hand it to him. The guy had nerve. He knew the launch was too big to run straight up onto the beach the way his little boat could, and was counting on the few minutes of delay while I got off the launch and onto the land after him to give him an edge.

"Panic can bring out unknown qualities in a man," philosophised Aunt Kathleen. She was taking all this very calmly, too calmly for my liking. But then, she wasn't in love with Elysia.

I noticed Aunt Kathleen looking around the deck speculatively. The little man was turning the launch now. Arturo's maneuver had opened some distance between us. The launch closed in rapidly on him. He was managing to keep ahead of us, though, and in a few minutes he'd be running his boat onto the beach, where we couldn't follow. I knelt on the side of launch near the stern, ready to jump out after Arturo.

Suddenly Aunt Kathleen saw what she was looking for. She pulled up a coil of rope from the deck and unrolled it rapidly, then started tying knots in one end of it. Keeping one eye on Arturo, I tried to figure out what she was up to. She must have remembered some Boy Scout lore from her guerilla days, because she was pretty fast with her knots. Now she was coiling the rope up again, and thrusting one arm through the coil. The launch suddenly came alongside Arturo's boat. I cheered inwardly. Maybe Pepe could swing around in front of him and cut him off. But the tide was helping Arturo now; despite his slower engine the lightness of his boat was carrying him forward neck and neck with the launch.

Suddenly a length of rope snaked out beside me and a noose settled neatly around Arturo's shoulders and arms. "Help me pull, Brian," shouted Aunt Kathleen.

She was standing beside me, one foot braced against a ledge that ran around the back of our deck. I grabbed the length of rope behind her and pulled so hard we both fell back on deck. The little man shut off his engine and started whooping with delight. We got to our knees, still clinging to the rope, and found our pull had yanked Arturo out of the boat into the water. The empty red boat was chug-chugging rapidly toward the beach while Arturo kicked and gasped beside the launch.

"Quick, Brian, the poor craytar is near destroyed with the water," cried Aunt Kathleen. We pulled steadily and gently, and the little man leaned over the side and gave our captive a hoist. In a minute he was on the deck, lying very still, his arms pinned to his sides by Aunt Kathleen's lasso, looking like a dead salmon. Only his dark eyes were alive, watching me with a terrified look. The little man knelt down beside him and wrapped a few more loops of rope around him, tying him securely.

"That was a fancy bit of rope-handling, Madame Commandant," I said.

"A trick I learned for Jim Riordan, a loyal son of Erin who came back to join our fight after six years in your Wild West," she said. "We used it to good effect on an unsuspecting peeler who wandered onto Fenit pier, County Kerry, just as we were landing a shipload of German arms."

The little man named Pepe said something in Spanish and jumped over the side of the launch. It was that we were almost back to the beach. The red boat, riderless now, was heading straight toward shore. Its nose plowed into the sand and stuck, lifting the stern out of the water. The motor buzzed away ineffectually in the sunny air for a few minutes, until Pepe waded up to it and shut it off. Then he inspected the rest of the boat for damage. The verdict must have been good, because he wore a bright smile as he waded back to his launch and pulled himself up over the side.

I looked at the beach. There were a few scattered bathers there, but our acrobatics with the rope didn't seem to have attracted an audience. Probably it had looked to them like a new form of water skiing. Still, if Aunt Kathleen had done what I told her, there *should* have been an audience. I turned to her accusingly.

"I told you to line up the cops," I said.

"Now, Brian, that would have been a very difficult matter, especially as I had no idea where the two of you were headed. It was only by sheer luck I caught sight of you boarding that bus at the very moment I found an adventurous cab driver."

I sighed. She was right. Then a pang of alarm struck me. "Where's Elysia?" I demanded. "You left her alone in the middle of a strange city!"

"What's your objection?" snapped Aunt Kathleen. "Since you're so hellfire sure that Arturo's the one who means her harm, what safer thing could she do than to take a cab back to the hotel nad wait for us there, as I told her to do? She'll be back there now, no doubt. I suggest the three of us join her. She'll be happy to learn of the safe conclusion of our chase."

"The three of us? You plan to bring Pepe along?"

"I said three, Brian, not four. Myself, yourself, and Arturo here."

"But surely the thing to do with Arturo is find the nearest cop and get him marched off to the slammer," I said.

"Don't be so precipitate, Brian."

"But you said yourself they've got a warrant out for him because of the chickens and Don Manuel's murder."

"That's true. And it's my intervention that led to that

warrant being issued. So it's my responsibility to see that an innocent man isn't caught in the toils of the law through my actions."

"Innocent!" I exploded. "Why, you yourself showed the cops . . ."

"I showed them the jewels, Brian. That was all." Her face was a stern mask of determination. "Arturo disappeared at that moment, to be sure, But that doesn't mean he was Don Manuel's murderer. He may have had other reasons to fear official investigation. Travelling with false papers, for instance." She cocked an eye toward Arturo, who was listening to us with intense concentration. He must have understood some English, because I could see the bit about false papers got through to him. He was staring at Aunt Kathleen with a strange mixture of hope and apprehension in his eyes.

"You're not going to turn him loose!"

"Of course not, Brian. We shall simply hold a hearing of our own, as we often did in the old days when a comrade was accused of working for the enemy. It's the only fair thing to do."

"You think he'll stand still for it?" I asked. "Perhaps we'd better bring Pepe along for reinforcement."

Aunt Kathleen turned to Arturo and began talking in rapid Spanish. I couldn't catch any of it except for a few names: Elysia, Don Manuel, Padre Hernandez. The mention of Elysia brought a sudden smile to the lean dark face; he relaxed and nodded enthusiastically as Aunt Kathleen continued to talk, then answered her in a few intense sentences. Finally she turned to me.

"I'm after telling him that the three of us will go back to the hotel and talk the whole business over in front of Elysia," he said. "I've assured him we're friends of Elysia's, first and foremost, and 'tis her welfare that means the most to us, not any bureaucratic nonsense about false papers or other minor illegalities."

"*Minor!*" I spluttered. "You call threatening to murder Elysia minor!"

"*Whisht*, Brian. There are many facets to this affair. Wait until you've heard the full story." Then, to my horror, she began to untie the knots that Pepe had tied.

"You aren't turning the bastard loose!" I exclaimed.

"He's bound by a stronger tie than rope, Brian. He's given me his word. I consider that sufficient." Her haughty gaze silenced me. I looked around for Pepe. But he was nodding in satisfaction.

"What goes on here? You've even bewitched Pepe into agreeing with your mad antics!"

"Pepe knows a gentleman when he sees one. The fact that Arturo gave his word to come with us quietly is enough for him."

"Are you all crazy? It's sure not enough for me!" I looked frantically up and down the beach. I saw a tan-uniformed figure up by the sea wall about half a block away. I head for the side of the boat, meanwhile rummaging through my mind for the necessary Spanish words. I thought "criminal" would come across all right, and "Captain Ramirez" might get me some mileage too. Anything to insure all our neat suspense-chase sequence didn't turn out to be wasted.

Aunt Kathleen stopped me. "Brian, I warn you, if you call the peelers in at this point, I'll never speak to you again." Her voice was hard and stern. I realized she was in dead earnest. "And what's more," she went on, "I can guarantee Elysia will never speak to you again. It's about time I explained one of the facts of life to you. This man who calls himself Arturo Urbino, is actually Elysia's brother, Alfredo Cantu Rodriguez."

That stopped me. I stood staring at the man in amazement. This sinister creep whom I had cast as the bad guy from the first hint of trouble was Elysia's brother? Then what did that make Elysia? I stared at Aunt Kathleen in horror. "O.K., Madame Commandant," I said, "I guess I'd better learn a little more about this. Let's get back to the Bolivar and get the whole mess sorted out."

Arturo, who had been watching me tensely, relaxed into a smile. Aunt Kathleen said a few words in Spanish to him. He nodded silently. She lifted the noose from his shoulders. The three of us climbed down onto the breakwater, where the boat was now moored. Little Pepe waved grateful goodbyes to all of us.

We headed for the Bolivar, three blocks away. If any of the people who passed us wondered why two men in sopping wet street clothes were escorting an elderly lady in a warm wool cape through the tropical afternoon of Veracruz, they were too polite to show it. We reached the Bolivar without incident and squished through the lobby. The room clerk gave us a startled glance, then went back to his newspaper. He was polite too.

The three of us headed for the stairs. A whole bunch of what a sloppier writer than I would call mixed feelings were churning inside of me. The keen analytic Singdahlsen mind, however, had no trouble sorting them out during the brief climb to the third floor. They were, in order of appearance:

(1) *Bewildermen:* The world had turned upside down. Arturo was a good guy. He was not threatening Elysia. He was not a mysterious stranger but Elysia's brother.

(2) *Chagrin:* How come Singdahlsen was so dumb as to go chasing after the good guy?

(3) *Horrible suspicion:* (a) Who *said* Arturo was a good guy? Just because he was Elysia's brother—maybe Elysia was working with the bad guys. Maybe she and Arturo had engineered Don Manuel's murder. Maybe she had thrown both me and Aunt Kathleen off the track with her story about being frightened. *OR* (b) *Maybe Aunt Kathleen was in on the plot and was one of the bad guys too!*

The Singdahlsen mental processes stopped spinning and came to a screeching halt. No! That was too much! Whatever else might change, Aunt Kathleen was my rock of sanity in a whirlpool of madness. I'd better just turn off the whole thinking machine before it got permanently fouled up, and wait for the promised revelation from Arturo's lips.

It didn't work. The wheels kept on clicking in my brain. I kept seeing Elysia's tense white face as she'd waited to leave the ship. There had been real fright in her eyes then. She wasn't pretending terror; someone *had* threatened her life.

But if it wasn't Arturo, who was it? A horrible feeling jolted my heart against my ribs. Elysia's enemy was still at large. While I'd been off splashing through the waves after her brother, with Aunt Kathleen following in my wake, the real killer had been handed a perfect opportunity. Aunt Kathleen had sent Elysia to the hotel to wait for us. What if someone else had found her first, alone and defenseless? Much as I wanted to see that beautiful face again, I felt an urgent hope that she'd disobeyed orders and was someplace far away from the Hotel Bolivar.

We had passed the second floor landing now, and were climbing the stairway leading to the third floor. Seething with anxiety, I hurried on ahead of the other two. Suddenly I froze in my tracks. A big bulky man with a soft felt hat pulled down over his eyes was leaning indolently against the door of the room Elysia and Aunt Kathleen shared. As we appeared, he suddenly straightened up, and shoved his right hand menacingly into his baggy coat pocket. I tensed in panic. Was this the unknown killer? Had we caught him in the nick of time?

I realized that *caught him* wasn't an accurate phrase to describe our current relationship with the big man. If that thing he was carrying in his coat pocket was a gun, *he* had caught *us*. I flicked a glance at Aunt Kathleen. She was *smiling*!

"*Buenos tardes,* Jose," she said sweetly, climbing past me to the corridor and advancing toward the big man with a hand outstretched in greeting.

The big man relaxed and smiled in reply. Aunt Kathleen had recognized him before I had. It was Jose, Raoul's bodyguard. Raoul must be inside. Inside with Elysia? But why? My brain started spinning again. Was Raoul part of the whole mess? Was he really a fugitive rebel, as Aunt Kathleen had claimed? Or just a common criminal on the run? Hiding out in his cabin, conning Father Hernandez into changing passports with him, acquiring a tough bruiser like Jose as a bodyguard—all that would have fitted the picture of a wanted criminal afraid of being arrested. Maybe *he* was someone out of Don Manuel's shadowy past, appearing on that fateful voyage to settle old scores. And hoodwinking a romantic-minded old lady and naive young intellectual.

Hoodwinking Aunt Kathleen! There the Singdahlsen mental apparatus stripped its gears and rattled to an abrupt stop. I did not think Aunt Kathleen was hoodwinkable.

Why then was she smiling at Jose? I noticed Arturo wasn't smiling. He looked puzzled and anxious. I could swear he had never laid eyes on Jose before. So they weren't confederates, anyway. But what was Raoul doing in the room with Elysia?

In the room with Elysia! Panic-stricken, I grabbed the knob, pushed past Aunt Kathleen who was still exchanging pleasantries with Jose, and flung myself into the room.

My imagination had heated up to the point where I wouldn't have been surprised to see her tied up and gagged with strips from the sheets, while Raoul stood over her with a lighted cigarette and an evil leer. Nothing of the kind. She and Raoul were sitting comfortably in the room's two armchairs. Elysia looked lovely and unruffled in a sleeveless blue dress that matched her eyes. They both looked startled at my sudden arrival. Then they both smiled. The atmosphere was positively cozy. It wouldn't have surprised me if Elysia had introduced Raoul as another of her long-lost brothers.

Then she looked over my shoulder and gave a little cry of delight. She jumped up and ran to Arturo, throwing her arms around him. His wet suit didn't seem to bother her. She clung to him, making little inarticulate sounds of joy. He did the same, in a more restrained fashion. "He'd *better* be her brother," I thought bitterly. The treatment Arturo was getting was exactly the kind of reception I'd been dreaming up for myself when I set off on my ill-fated knight-errantry.

Meanwhile, Raoul had risen to his feet. He did his little dance of greeting for Aunt Kathleen, and said "*A sus ordenes.*" Aunt Kathleen and he went off into a torrent of Spanish, for which she emerged in a few minutes to explain, "He's telling me what a charming young lady Elysia is, and how pleased he is to make her acquaintance."

"That's supposed to be my line," I snapped. "What the hell is he doing here, anyway?" Relieved as I was to see Elysia safe and unperturbed, I wasn't very happy about the instant friendship my ex-roommate seemed to have established with her.

Aunt Kathleen looked surprised at my waspish tone. "Why, naturally, he came in answer to my invitation, Brian. You don't suppose he'd barge in here without being asked, do you? As a matter of fact, I have favor to request of him."

I was all through with supposing at the moment. I wanted some facts. But if I knew Aunt Kathleen, she had to take her own time about producing them. So I shut up and let her go on talking.

"The man we call Raoul has just been saying how sorry he was to read of the death of the priesteen. He feels very guilty about it. I told him to hold his tears the while, til he hears Arturo's story."

"*Arturo's* story! What's Arturo got to do with Raoul and Father Hernandez?"

"Patience, my dear Brian. We've a tangled web to unravel. There's no use rushing our fences. I suggest we all find a comfortable seat and a glass of something to soothe our nerves. Meanwhile, do you think you could provide a change of costume for this poor damp gossoon?"

Clearly, if we were ever go get down to the cold hard facts that would dispel my bewilderment, I would have to play the game her way. I exited dutifully to my next-door room, changed into a pair of dry jeans and a shirt, and picked up another set for Arturo. I returned to the conference room and found Aunt Kathleen beaming at five stemmed glasses lined up before her on the dressing table. I tossed the dry clothes to Arturo. He smiled gratefully and retired to the bathroom to change. Aunt Kathleen flourished a squat bottle with an unfamiliar label.

"Since this promises to be a memorable occasion, it's a fitting time to break out this fine old bottle of port my dear Fergus bought from Mitchell's in Kildare Street, Dublin City, our last Christmas together. He was always a great man for the telling of stories, he being a journalist and all, God rest his soul. But I'll warrant he never told a stronger tale than the one we're about to hear."

Arturo emerged from the bathroom, looking sleek and elegant even though my pants were too short for him. I wondered why the clothes looked so different on me. Aunt Kathleen had filled all the glasses with a tawny liquid and handed one to each of us. Arturo accepted the fifth glass with a little bow. Aunt Kathleen raised hers so that it sparkled in the afternoon sunshine pouring in from the outside balcony. "Oil for the tongue of the bard," she said. "Now Arturo, you tell your story in whatever words you fancy, and I'll translate it all for Brian as it flows from your lips."

CHAPTER 9

"First, I must tell you something about our family, Elysia's and mine," Arturo began, with Aunt Kathleen murmuring a quiet translation in my ear, like those headphones at the U.N. General Assembly. "My father, Don Rafael Cantu, was a very strong man, a very intelligent man, a very powerful man. But he was not a good man."

Elysia's eyes filled with pain, and she glanced at me as if she wanted to make sure I understood what her brother was saying. Warmed by this evidence that she remembered my existence, I tried to look reassuring.

"It is difficult to say these things to strangers," continued Arturo "but they must be said. Besides, my sister has just assured me that *Señora* O'Connell and Mr. Singdahlsen are not strangers, but good friends, who have been of much help and comfort under trying circumstances. As I was saying, Don Rafael Cantu was not a good man. He owned an importing business in Cadiz which might in itself have supplied his family with enough to be comfortable, but enough was not enough for him. He wanted great wealth and power. So behind the mask of his legal business, he began conducting many illegal activities. I could not escape knowing about these activities, though I tried to keep the knowledge from my mother and sister. Even so, when he had been drinking he would boast to us all of his criminal exploits, which went undetected and unpunished during his lifetime. He is in the hands of God now, so I will not blacken his name further. You can imagine for yourselves the sort of enterprises that may shelter under the cover of an importing business, especially one situated so close to North Africa.

"So much for his public life. In private, he was a tyrant showing no love for his family. He made rude and overbearing to our mother and sometimes beat her unmercifully. She was always meek and submissive, and from an early age she taught us to listen to his insults, his bragging about his misdeeds, and his scorn for his wife and children without showing anger. This was difficult, as you may imagine, especially after our mother died. We felt her early death was caused by despair over his coldness and brutality. He exulted over her death in front of us, celebrating it as a victory over her whole family. She was a Rodriquez, you see; she came from a higher social level than he did. To us, these distinctions meant nothing. To him, they still rankled, he never tired when she was alive of rubbing her nose in the fact that her brother, who had been Don Rafael's partner during his younger days, had also carried on criminal activities, until Don Rafael had turned on him and cheated him out of his fair share of the proceeds. Her brother, our uncle, had left Spain a ruined man. Even though he also was a criminal, Elysia and I honored him as our father's enemy and the brother of our dear mother. Those years of suppressed rage strengthened our resolve to make good someday the harm our father had done him."

"Rodriguez!" I said, suddenly remembering. "Any relation to—"

"Yes," said Arturo, "Don Manuel Rodriguez Acosta

was our uncle. He came to Mexico and made another fortune of his own to replace the wealth Don Rafael had cheated him of. He often came to Cadiz on business trips. I tried several times to meet him and tell him we were on his side, but because of his hatred for my father, he refused to see me. Finally my father became very sick and the doctor told him he would die soon. We had heard Don Manuel was in Cadiz again, and my father begged me to bring his former partner to his deathbed, so he could make restitution. It was while I was unsuccessfully pleading with Don Manuel in the dining room of his hotel to honor my father's dying wish that Elysia first met Father Hernandez.''

I stared at Elysia. She gave a tremulous little smile. Father Hernandez! So he'd been on the scene even before the *Virgen* sailed! Had Aunt Kathleen's dark suspicions been valid after all?

"My father's illness became rapidly worse during my absence," continued Arturo. "He became frightened and told Elysia to summon a priest to hear his confession. She phoned the priest of our parish, but he was not at home. Frantically, she rushed out in the street, hoping to find a priest at a nearby boys' school. As luck would have it, she met a young man in a cassock only a block away from our house, and told him of the emergency. He instantly agreed to come with her and talk with my father. He introduced himself as Father Julio Hernandez, saying he was a Mexican priest visiting Spain to raise money for his order.

"When I came home, unhappy and frustrated because Don Manuel had sent me away in anger, Elysia met me with good news—or so we thought at the time. She told me my father had made his confession to the priest, and afterwards had called her in to witness his signature to a document. In her presence, my father gave the priest a paper he said was the deed to a piece of land he owned in the Dominican Republic. The document he signed was meant to transfer this deed to Don Manuel. He told Elysia there was "something valuable" buried on this land, "under the stones" as he put it, that would repay the debt he owed to Don Manuel.

"By the time I got home, my father was in a coma, unconscious, so I could not ask him what he meant by 'something valuable,' but I knew enough about his activities to make a good guess. I knew he had acquired, through his private channels, a large amount of gold bullion which he could not legally display. I guessed some of this gold was buried on that lot in the Dominical Republic.

"According to Elysia, the priest had promised to seek out Don Manuel and deliver the deed to him in person. She said there was a provison in the document she witnessed that gave Father Hernandez the legal responsibility of doing this. We were both very glad that our father, or his own accord, had cancelled out his debt to our uncle. When he died a few hours later, we did not shed many tears, but we resolved that he should have a suitable funeral.

"We set out immediately for the cathedral, to make arrangements for the funeral. This was only four days before the *Virgen de Toluca* sailed. If you remember, the *Fiesta de los Reyes Catolicos* was in progress. The streets and bars were full of excited people, drinking and singing. There was a feeling of abandon in the air.

"As we passed one of the bars, Elysia suddenly stopped abruptly, with a strange look on her face." He nodded toward his sister to continue.

"I recognized a voice," said Elysia. "I looked inside the bar to be sure. I was right. It was the man who had called himself Father Hernandez. But now he was not wearing his cassock. He had obviously been drinking heavily, and was talking loudly, saying terrible things . . ." She shook her head helplessly and her voice trailed off.

"He was blaspheming," said Arturo. "Neither Elysia or I are ardent Catholics, but we respect a priest who practices his religion. Obviously, this priest did not. He was making dirty jokes about the Holy Virgin, mostly the same old chestnuts I'd heard at school, but he finished with a new one. 'I'm the Virgin's pimp,' he bragged. 'She'll bring me a fortune in gold before the end of this month.' Then he laughed uproariously, clearly finding some secret meaning in his own words.

"We were both shaken. Was this the man whom my father had entrusted with his deathbed wish? We were convinced he was an imposter, not a priest at all. When we got home again, after making arrangements for the funeral, I asked Elysia to try to remember exactly what the document she'd witnessed had said.

"She told me it was written in the so-called priest's handwriting, and consisted of three pages. She tried to remember the exact words written on each page. Suddenly she turned to me, horror-stricken."

"I'd realized the trick the priest had played on my father," interrupted Elysia. "The first page said that he was entrusting the deed to Father Hernandez. The *second* page said the priest was to see that the deed was transferred to Don Manuel Rodriguez Acosta in payment of an old debt. The third page gave the priest 'all legal power necessary to conduct this business.' I suddenly realized that if the second page was removed, the document would read as though the dead was being given to Father Hernandez himself."

"You can imagine how horrified we were," Arturo went on. "I immediately tried to see Don Manuel again, but the hotel told me he had gone to Madrid for a few days, and would not return until the day he was due to sail on the *Virgen de Toluca*. The ship's name reminded me immediately of the imposter's boast that the Virgin would bring him gold. In a flash I guessed that he meant that the ship would take him to my father's gold in the Dominican Republic. I realized there was no time to lose."

I managed to get a question in. "Couldn't you have gone to the police?" I asked.

"Brian, you're obsessed with the coppers," said Aunt Kathleen. What would be the point of going to the Spanish police to safeguard a buried treasure of illegal gold in another country?"

Arturo smiled at Aunt Kathleen gratefully. "Exactly," he said. "At the time, remember, we were not concerned with keeping the gold for ourselves. We were intent on righting an old wrong by putting it in the hands of our uncle, Don Manuel. Obviously, our only hope of doing that lay in retrieving the document and the deed from the fake priest.

"I found out from the business agent for the *Virgen de Toluca*, a man who had often been bribed by my father to provide him with information, that Father Hernandez had indeed booked a passage on the ship. I made use of some other shady connections to secure a passport and book a passage under the false name of Arturo Urbino, so as not to take the risk of alarming the priest by appearing under my father's family name. I told Elysia nothing of this, but she guessed what I was up to."

"I couldn't let Alfredo go after the false priest alone," Elysia broke in. "I would have died of worry, sitting there at home in Candiz and wondering what was happening to him. So I booked a passage too, without telling Alfredo. Of course, since the priest already knew me, I had to travel under my own name."

"You can imagine how alarmed I was to see her in the ship's dining room that first night out," said Arturo. "I knew she was in infinitely more danger that I was. Hernandez didn't know me. He did know Elysia. I don't know whether he knew when he booked his passage that Don Manuel was sailing on the same voyage, but once aboard, he must have realized that the combination of Elysia and Don Manuel meant trouble for his plan to keep the gold for himself.''

"I wasn't very clever," said Elysia. "When Father Hernandez approached me that night, I tried to pretend I was simply escaping from the sorrow of my father's death by taking a pleasure cruise. I'm not a good liar. He didn't believe me. He said some very ugly things to me. I lost my head and called him an imposter. Then he became *really* angry at me. He threatened to kill me if I said anything at all to Don Manuel or anyone else about him."

"*That* was the argument I fell into the middle of," I said.

"Yes. When you appeared out of the darkness, Father Hernandez got even angrier. He was afraid you had heard enough of our quarrel to be dangerous to him."

"Wow!" I said. "And then, the very next morning he saw me talking with Don Manuel."

"That really frightened him," said Elysia. "He came to my cabin and told me the gringo who had overheard our conversation the night before was talking to Don Manuel. He thought you hadn't said anything yet about him to Don Manuel, since you both seemed to be in good mood, but he was afraid you'd try to get more details from me. He warned me he'd kill us both if he saw me talking to you. That's why I left so quickly when you sat down beside us that morning. I was terrified. I managed to see Alfredo secretly, and told him what was happening. When we all went ashore at Tenerife, he kept an eye on Father Hernandez and warned me when he headed our way.''

''And I thought you were a jealous boyfriend,'' I said to Arturo. He smiled. Elysia blushed.

''My soul from the devil, Brian,'' said Aunt Kathleen suddenly. ''I've just remembered some bits of the colloquy we had with the priesteen in Tenerife. We put our collective foot in it, right enough.''

I looked blank.

''Don't you remember, you were airing your grand knowledge of old Spanish proverbs,'' she said.

The light dawned. ''The habit doesn't make the monk!'' I groaned. ''What a moment to pull that one out of the hat!''

''And then I had to made a remark about fine feathers and fine birds.''

''And then I topped it off by mentioning gold,'' I said. ''The bastard must have thought we knew all about his scheme—both the hocus pocus about the deed, and the designs he had on those diamond—stuffed chickens.''

''Wait a minute, Brian. He had no way of knowing about the jewels in those chickens' crops at that time.''

''I'm not too sure,'' I said. ''How come he had already made up that Saint Francis story to explain his hanging around the cages?''

''Maybe he just wanted to keep an unobtrusive eye on Don Manuel.''

''He would have been wiser to avoid him completely,'' said Arturo. ''I agree with Mr. Singdahlsen. I think he already knew about the jewel smuggling. It might be my father mentioned it in making his confession.''

''Our father knew about the smuggling?'' asked Elysia, wide-eyed.

"The method was his own invetntion. He and Don Manuel had used it when they were partners. It might easily have been one of the long catalog of sins he confessed to the false priest. When the imposter heard that Don Manuel was bringing a cargo of fighting cocks with him, he could have jumped to the conclusion that he was still using our father's old tricks. Certainly he learned about the chickens at some point. Why else would he have made that last-minute offer to buy them from me after Don Manuel's murder?"

"We're getting ahead of our story, lad," said Aunt Kathleen reprovingly.

"The next act of this little drama was the attack on me, I think."

Arturo and Elysia turned startled faces toward me.

"They haven't heard about that yet," said Aunt Kathleen. Then she explained in Spanish to them about the deck-lurker's frustrated attempt to knife me. Elysia gave a little cry of distress. Arturo looked grave.

"You have been in great danger for our sakes, Mr. Singdahlsen. I'm glad the assassin was not successful."

I looked at Aunt Kathleen with new respect. "You *told* me we two were the only passengers who knew about that attack. That was after you had picked up Father Hernandez's slip in mentioning *two* attacks. But I was so starry-eyed I wouldn't take you seriously."

"I wasn't completely convinced myself of his guilt at that point. You notice we're still calling him *Father* Hernandez. Even without his cassock, the aura of the priesthood made a strong shield against suspicion.'

"And then when he made that noble offer to Raoul . . ." I said.

"All in due time, Brian, all in due time. Let's get back to the story. The evening after that attack on Brian was the night of the dance. You came up to Don Manuel, Alfredo, and lured him away somehow."

I blinked. It was hard to follow her switch to calling Elysia's brother by his real name. To me he would always be Arturo.

"He was angry when he saw me." The lean dark face grew somber as he thought of the murdered man. "I told him quickly that I was speaking for myself, not my dead father, and that I had come to warn him of danger. He became interested and listened to me. I told him of the deed, the gold, and the document the false priest was carrying. I told him of the threats to Elysia. I warned him the priest might intend harm to him as well. After all, the simplest way for the imposter to make sure Don Manuel did not contest his possession of the deed would be to kill him. He became convinced, and accepted my offer to act as his bodyguard. Just in time, too. It was that same evening that Hernandez made the attack on him I had predicted. Luckily, I was waiting nearby, and prevented any harm to Don Manuel."

"But Hernandez got away from you," I said.

"I let him get away. Don Manuel and I had already discussed the possibility of denouncing the priest as an imposter. We agreed that the time was not ripe. As you say, *Señora* O'Connell, the aura of the priesthood makes a good shield. Who would take the word of an unknown young man travelling on false papers against the word of a popular priest? Once ashore, we might have been able to prove he was not what he claimed to be. On board ship, in the middle of the Atlantic . . ." He shrugged his shoulders expressively.

"They would have listened to Don Manuel," I objected.

"Possibly. But if Hernandez had been challenged, the question of motive would have come up. That might have meant disclosing the existence of the gold—illegal gold, you remember. Don Manuel did not wish to endanger his chances of laying hands on my father's be-quest to him."

I nodded. "I can see his point," I said. "Anyway, you must have put up a pretty good fight. It convinced our con artist friend to lay off the monkey business."

Arturo looked confused. Aunt Kathleen translated. Arturo smiled. "I *was* a little rough with him. Furthermore, the ship's captain was sufficiently concerned to mount a watch over Don Manuel. The assassin must have realized he had no chance of a successful attack on board ship. That was why he bided his time until he was able to lure Don Manuel ashore in San Juan."

"Wait a minute," I said. "First I want to know about the day in Santo Domingo. Why were you shadowing us that day?"

"Oh, that. Naturally, Don Manuel and I were worried that the imposter might make an attempt to remove the treasure from the lot my father had given Don Manuel. It would have been a clever move. Then he could have proved his innocence by handing over the deed to Don Manuel, as promised. The land itself would have been relatively worthless, compared to the gold. And of course, Don Manuel could not have afforded to ask questions about gold that didn't legally exist. On Don Manuel's instructions, I followed the false priest to prevent any attempt to move the gold. Fortunately, *Senora* O'Connell and yourself accompanied him the treasure site, so there was no need for me to intervene."

"How about that, *Madame Commandant,*" I said, turning to Aunt Kathleen. "What were *you* up to that day? Don't tell me you were already sitting on the secret of the gold . . ."

"Not at all, Brian. I was merely intrigued. My observations had led me to credit Don Manuel with a great deal of acumen, and since Alfredo here was obviously following his orders, I realized the old man was suspicious of the alleged priest. Since I already had my own suspicions, I felt it might be interesting to assist Alfredo in his shadowing assignment."

"All right then, what had made *you* suspicious? I know you gave me a whole string of reasons later on . . ."

"Most of which occurred to me well after Don Manuel's murder. I had given little thought to what the priesteen's game might be up to that time. The day we landed in Santo Domingo, there was only one detail of his behavior that led me to suspect him of hanky panky. The business of the breviary."

"The breviary?"

"The little black book he read his daily prayers from. You may have noticed it had a ribbon in it to use as a place marker."

"So?"

"In my wide acquaintance with members of the clergy from many countries, I have learned something about the breviary, which except for language is the same in all countries. The prayers for each day are arranged in a chronological sequence, beginning with the start of the church year in November. And yet, in the middle of March, the priest kept his place marker near the front of the breviary. If he had *really* been reading the prayers assigned for March, the marker would have been nearer the center of the book. When I noticed that, I knew there was something fishy about the priest. Alfredo's obvious shadowing of him spurred me into a closer enquiry into what shenanigans he might be up to."

Arturo had been listening to her explanation attentively. "I understand," he said. "I wondered at the time why you appeared so providentially to assist me in thwarting any attempt by Hernandez to move the gold. I do not know if he might actually have tried to do so, if you had not been there."

"As it was, he was happy enough to spot the 'stones'

Don Rafael had mentioned, I'll warrant," said Aunt Kathleen.

"The hearth of his ancestors," I groaned. "What a pretty little piece of sentimental hogwash!"

"Don't blame yourself for being taken in, Brian. He was a foxy rogue, and I daresay had fooled many a person as astute as yourself during his checkered career."

"Don Manuel was very pleased to hear my news," said Arturo. "He felt sure that since the imposter had been unable to move the gold, the danger was over. He said that once he and the chickens were safely back in Mexico, he could take steps to expose the supposed priest if he tried to press his claim."

"The old man had told you about the chickens?" asked Aunt Kathleen.

"Yes. He'd done that the day after I saved him from the assassin's knife. He, too, thought Hernandez showed a suspicious interest in the fighting cocks, and felt I should be fully informed of anything that might prove dangerous to him. Of course, we realized that if Father Hernandez *did* know the secret of the diamonds, it would not be wise to expose him before the evidence of Don Manuel's smuggling was safely through customs. We thought there would be plenty of time to catch up with the fake priest, once on land."

"But the waiting turned out to be more dangerous than he thought," I said.

Arturo shook his head sadly. "It was unfortunate that among my false papers, I had not been able to obtain a Mexican visa. I was very unhappy about leaving Don Manuel, even for an hour, to go the Mexican consulate in Puerto Rico. If I had been with him, he would never have allowed himself to be lured ashore by that phone call."

"Phone call! I thought he went ashore with Father Hernandez!" I said.

"That was a lie the imposter told the police. He probably intended to cover himself in case anyone had seen him with Don Manuel in San Juan. I knew better. On my return, I found a message for me in Don Manuel's cabin, to which he had given me the key. It said, 'Called away on important business—S.D.' I immediately assumed someone had phone him, pretending to have information about the land in Santo Domingo that he could not reveal over the phone. Why my uncle did not realize the assassin was setting a trap for him, I do not know. Perhaps his hunger for gold overruled his common sense. At any rate, he was gone. I learned from his cabin steward that he had indeed received a phone call from the shore and left the ship immediately. That was the last anyone ever saw of him—until the police fished his body out of the harbor."

"Didn't the police question the cabin steward?"

"I suppose so. No doubt he claimed to know nothing. Anything would seem better to an antlike creature of that sort than to be involved in a murder investigation."

"You told us he sent you a message to have the captain sail without him."

"I know. That was a lie. But when the hours passed and Don Manuel did not return, I felt sure he was in trouble. Finally, when I saw Hernandez come calmly up the gangplank with a satisfied smile on his face, I was convinced there was nothing I could do to help Don Manuel. He was already dead. The false priest had eliminated the rightful owner of the deed."

"You could have put the police to work catching his murderer," I said.

"Could I? Again, who would believe me? An unknown young man, travelling with false papers, accusing a priest of the Church? I was sure if I tried to raise an alarm, the assassin would immediately betray the secret of the chickens and accuse me of murdering my employer in order to secure the proceeds of that smuggling scheme.''

"A tangled web indeed," murmured Aunt Kathleen. "What about that power of attorney you showed the ship's captain?"

"That was genuine," said Arturo bitterly. "After the attack on the deck, Don Manuel had insisted on writing out that power of attorney for me in his own handwriting, in case anything should happen to him. It was a bitter moment when I found myself forced to use it to forestall an investigation of his murder. But I felt I had no choice."

"By that time you knew Hernandez knew that you were suspicious of him," I said. "Weren't you worried that he might attack *you* next?"

"A little. But I had been more than a match for him already. I was more worried about Elysia. After all, Hernandez did not know that I had a personal stake in avenging Don Manuel's murder. He did not know I was his nephew. He probably thought I was merely a paid bodyguard, perhaps with criminal connections, who would not wish to risk an investigation of Don Manuel's death. He did not think I even knew about the treasure the fighting cocks carried, otherwise he would not have had the effrontery to make that ridiculous offer to buy them from me before we landed. But he *knew* Elysia was Don Manuel's niece, and that she could give the police a firm motive that would point to him as the murderer. I thought she would be his next victim. So I managed to get a note to her saying not to leave her cabin or talk to anyone before we got to Veracruz."

"I had already seen enough of Father Hernandez's anger to be terrified," said Elysia. "I spent a terrible three days huddled in my bed listening to every little sound outside my door. It was such a relief when *Tia Catalina* pushed her way in."

I blinked. *Tia Catalina*? Then I saw the smug smile on Aunt Kathleen's face. Of course, I should have realized she had acquired a niece as well as a nephew on the trip. "Back to your story, lad," she said to Arturo.

"Why were you shadowing Father Hernandez in Caracus?" I asked.

"For lack of anything better to do. I had no idea at that point of what to do next. I felt as long as I kept an eye on the pretender, I could ward off any unexpected attack on me or my sister."

"Meanwhile I was happily installing the good father in a niche just a few notches lower than Jesus Christ," I lamented. "In spite of all the evidence you threw at me, madame commandant, I thought he was a good guy. And that noble offer to Raoul to exchange passports clinched it."

"I must admit, that self-sacrificing gesture threw the dust in my eyes for a time," said Aunt Kathleen. "You see, Elysia had admitted to me she was mortally afraid, but she was still too terrified to tell me just who she was afraid of."

"That aura of the priesthood," said Elysia, shaking her head. "In spite of the fact that I knew he was an imposter, the world 'padre' summoned up all my schoolgirl memories of priests as superhuman beings who knew my every thought and deed."

"Hindsight in a great thing," said Aunt Kathleen. "As we sit here in peace and quiet, I can think of many reasons it would be to the sham priest's advantage to enter Mexico under another passport than his own. That photograph the police took of him, for instance. Enough to make any criminal nervous. No doubt the spalpeen was shaking his boots lest some old acquantance in the Mexican police see it and arrange a special welcome for him. 'tis eminently possible he's already known to them as a defrauder of women and orphans."

"That's guesswork," I said.

"Of course. All my conclusions about the priest—and the chickens—were based on guesswork. I was planning to put my guesses to the test immediately after our feet touched dry land."

"You sure left no room for guessing so far as the chickens were concerned," I said admiringly.

"I verified my guess about the priest as well," said Aunt Kathleen. "I made a phone all on my way to the hotel yesterday to an official of the Church in Mexico City. It took him no time at all to assure me that the order 'Father Hernandez' claimed to be collecting money for didn't exist. He was very interested, by the way. Made me give him a detailed description of the *furrier,* and then told me they'd had an enquiry from Malta about a Mexican priest soliciting funds there. Another name, but the description fitted our man. He must have been posing as a priest for a long time before fate dropped something even more lucrative into his lap."

I stared at her accusingly. "Yesterday! And you didn't say a word to me?"

"Would it have made a difference, Brian?"

"Of course! It would have cleared up the whole mystery. I would have known Father Hernandez was the bad guy, and Arturo and I wouldn't have had to get sopping wet," I said aggrievedly.

"And if today's performance is any guide, you would have insisted on barging right down to the peelers with the information," she said acidly.

"Of course. They could have nabbed the phony priest right away!"

"Perhaps. But could they have convicted him? There was no real evidence to connect him with Don Manuel's murder. At that point I wasn't absolutely sure myself he was the murderer."

"If they'd found that deed and the document . . ." I said.

"I didn't know that part of the story until Elysia finally broke down and told me the whole thing while you were out to breakfast this morning."

"Well, you should have told me this morning," I insisted.

"I know," said Aunt Kathleen. "I should have. Especially after I learned that Alfredo had tried to see us. I realized the poor man must be going mad with frustration because my cunning precautions had kept him from getting in touch with his sister. But when you dropped that bombshell about Father Hernandez's death, I felt I needed time to think through all the implications."

"Implications!" I groaned. "The implications were simple. The bad guy, the guy out for Elysia's neck, was out of the picture. We could all have relaxed and stopped worrying."

"No, we couldn't. We had a new problem to solve—the problem of who killed Father Hernandez."

"That's no problem," I said scornfully. "Obviously, his con man's trick of switching passports backfired on him."

Raoul had straightened up in his chair and was listening to us intently. He shook his head sorrowfully when Aunt Kathleen translated to him my comments about "backfiring."

"How ironic!" he said in Spanish. "He escaped the law but fell a victim to my enemies."

"Did he now? I wonder," said Aunt Kathleen, so cryptically I could have kicked her. "Perhaps you can enlighten us further on that point, Alfredo."

Arturo was staring at the floor. He looked at Elysia for a moment, than at Aunt Kathleen. Then he sighed a deep sigh and pulled an envelope from his pocket. He unfolded a yellowed parchment and three sheets of crisp white paper with some writing on them, and handed them to Aunt Kathleen.

"Ah, yes. The deed and the document. So you brought the sad story to an end," she said. Arturo was silent.

"I expected something of the sort when I learned you were Elysia's brother," said Aunt Kathleen. "Especially remembering that you and our holy imposter disappeared at the same moment. You followed him, I suppose?"

"I followed him," said Arturo. "I followed him all day. He thought he was safe. Perhaps he counted on your finding the diamonds to put me into the hands of the police. At any rate, he didn't notice I was following him. He drank a great deal, and became careless. I confronted him, we fought, and I killed him with his own knife. I did not know whether I was doing right or wrong. I still do not know. I only know I could not bear to see that villain thwart my father's dying wish and kill my uncle, and yet go unpunished." He took a deep breath, then stood quietly, staring down at the floor as though waiting for our verdict.

"Justice is a slippery beast, Alfredo," said Aunt Kathleen in a softer voice than I had ever heard her use. "I still lie awake some nights, thinking of the verdicts I cast my vote on years ago, when we had to pass judgment on informers. You did the best you knew. It's all any of us can do."

Arturo raised his head and looked at her. They exchanged a long look. I felt very young and naive and out of things.

Finally Raoul broke the silence. With a keen glance at Aunt Kathleen he said, "I think I can guess why you asked me here. This young man is in a dangerous position."

"The police want to question him about those diamonds," said Aunt Kathleen. "If they find him, the fact that he's Don Manuel's nephew, travelling on false papers, won't help at all."

"They make link me with the death of the so-called priest, too," said Arturo. "Some of the passengers may remember that he spent a great deal of time watching the fighting cocks."

"I have an idea the peelers won't be lepping with impatience to investigate that bowsie's death, Alfredo. I've already passed on the information about his little masquerade. I also took the liberty of suggesting they check his fingerprints against their file of wanted criminals."

"I, too, may be able to dampen their zeal as regards that murder," said Raoul. "My friends here have friends among the police. I can see that word reaches them that I was the intended target. That should ensure the whole case being smothered in a discreet silence. Meanwhile, I suggest the safest course for this young man is to leave the country immediately."

Arturo looked at him despairingly. "Of course, you will need another passport," added Raoul. "The officials will be looking for Arturo Urbino. My friends can help in this matter also. If you will give me your correct passport, I'm sure it can be exchanged for another one. We can also arrange to get you out of the country on a plane headed for Cuba, if you wish. Once there, you are very near Santo Domingo."

Arturo's desperate eyes filled with hope. "The new passport would solve my problems," he said. "I don't know how to thank you."

"I shall regard it as a favor to my good comrade,

Senora O'Connell,'' said Raoul. ''The passport will be in your hands tonight. I notice you haven't commented on my suggestion about the flight to Cuba.''

''I'm . . . I'm not sure whether or not I want the gold in Santo Domingo,'' said Arturo. ''I wanted Don Manuel to have it. For myself—perhaps it would be better to burn the deed and let the gold lie there forever.''

''What nonsense!'' snorted Aunt Kathleen, synchronizing neatly with Raoul's muttered, ''*Que tonto*!''

''My father came by that gold dishonestly,'' said Arturo. ''I am capable of earning an honest living for myself.''

''So am I,'' said Elysia determinedly.

''Babes in the woods,'' said Aunt Kathleen. ''You remind me of the highminded arguments Brendan Callahan put up when our unit found the garrison's payroll in an armored car we ambushed near Cashel, County Tipperary. 'Sure, we're patriots, not robbers,' he kept saying. 'It's tainted money. Let's leave the cash for them it belongs to.' The rest of us finally convinced him we could use the guns that tainted money would buy.''

''You think I should take the gold?'' asked Arturo uncertainly.

''The secret's out, lad. You're not the only one now who knows it's there. For all we know, the false priest may have passed a tip to a pal of his. I daresay our friend Raoul will be after it for his revolution if you don't take it first. I might even decide to do a bit of digging myself. No customs official has ever examined my carpet bag. A bar of gold bullion would make a tidy start toward endowing a fund for impoverished authors.'' She smiled sweetly at me.

''I'm not sure I'd risk getting myself or my friends in trouble with the Dominican government,'' said Raoul.

"But if you cared to make a substantial donation to our party, we would accept it gratefully. It would balance out all the money your late uncle bestowed on our enemies."

Arturo still looked uncertain. "Elysia and I must discuss this," he said. "Meanwhile, Cuba is as good a destination as any. You can be sure that if I do decide to take the gold, I will not forget how all of you have helped us."

"The gold's still illegal," I blurted. "I mean, you can't sell it on the open market."

Arturo looked at me with an ironic smile. "I am finding it difficult to break with my father's criminal past," he said. "I may as well continue to use some of his old friends for my purpose."

"That's the ticket, lad. What your father got by foul means, you can use for your own fair ends."

"Perhaps," said Arturo.

"Aunt Kathleen," I said. "You're very free and easy now about ignoring legal regulations. Why did you take all that trouble to expose the diamond smuggling scheme? Did you think it would help Elysia somehow?"

"Help Elysia? I thought it wouldn't hurt. You must remember, I didn't know then who you were, Alfredo. Elysia didn't trust me enough to tell me. There was still a possibility that you were as dangerous to Elysia as Brian insisted you were. I thought exposing the diamond smuggling scheme might serve to remove you neatly from the scene, thus cutting down on our list of suspects. But I must admit," she said, a familiar roguish twinkle in her eyes, "that the main reason was just to have a bit of a lark. It was great fun to see all those customs men squawking and running in circles, and they looking like a bunch of well-fed chickens themselves."

"My dear auntie," I said. "You're a very dangerous

travelling companion."

She cocked an eyebrow at me. "You're too sober, Brian. It's time to forget the perilous past and drink to the glorious future." Deftly, she emptied the bottle of port into our glasses.

"*Salud, dinero y amor, y tiempo para gastarlos,*" she said softly. I looked at Elysia as I drank. She looked back demurely over the top of the glass. There was no fear in her eyes now.

"The waiter from Hoboken taught me that one too," I said. "Health, wealth and love, and time to enjoy them."

Elysia's smile deepened. "You understand berry well the Spanish," she said.

Flores Magon 1379
Veracruz, Ver.
MEXICO
31st May 197-

Dear Peter,

Enclosed, my latest brainchild. It will surprise you, I think. It will perturb even old imperturbable Peter. "What, the Great White Hope for a new age of satire writing thrillers!" you will say. All right, publish it under a pseudonym. I need money, not glory.

The ms. will tell you what's been happening. A few additional notes, which you can add to the last chapter if you like. (Hell, you're an editor. Earn your keep.)

The phony priest turned out to have a criminal record, just as Aunt Kathleen had predicted. Nothing more appeared in the press about the corpse carrying Raoul's passport. Arturo-Alfredo got out of the country safely. We just received a postcard saying he's enjoying his holiday in Santo Domingo.

Lots of postcards today. One from Raoul, too, saying he's enjoying his holiday in Havana, and asking us to give his regards to Aunt Kathleen.

That redoubtable lady reached New York somehow. She didn't give the details. I suspect she made part of the trip by ox cart. She sent us a picture of the O'Connell grandchild, with a cryptic message on the back reading, "Mountains don't meet, people do." I figure I haven't seen the last of her.

Just before she left Veracruz, I taxed her again with her cavalier disregard of legal regulations concerning gold bullion. "But Brian, lad," she said, "since I saw you were hellbent to marry an heiress, I had to do my best to see you married a really rich one."

Thus far, Elysia hasn't shown any great inclination to leap into marriage. She's friendly enough, though, and appears content to stay here in Veracruz indefinitely. My Spanish is improving at a miraculous rate.

That new book I started on the boat sits in a drawer in our *casita,* waiting for Singdahlsen's literary renaissance, which seems to be a long time coming. I'm sitting on the beach, having given in and written truth that sounds like fiction, rather than fiction too close to the truth. I'm still groping for direction. But the sea is calm, the palm trees are graceful, and sun is hot, and I see Elysia coming along the sand toward me. I figure my identity crisis can wait a few months more. Or years. Or forever. As Aunt Kathleen would say, "'Twill be all the same in a hundred years."

Salud, amigo!
Brian